Away on the Range

By Fletcher Newbern

A Personalized
Romance Novel
Featuring
Beth Butts
and
Mike Butts

Published By
yournovel.com
Beach House Presentations
3100 Arrowwood Drive
Raleigh, NC 27604
© 2000 by Fletcher Newbern

This Book Is Lovingly Dedicated To

Mike Butts
From
Beth

Happy Valentine's Day
February 14, 2008

CHAPTER ONE

The Triple Z Airport was small, indeed, especially when compared to Baltimore where Beth and Mike had left so many hours earlier on this much-needed vacation. The six-seater Cessna had been the final leg of their air passage, and now as the landing strip was in sight, the whole sky seemed to be lit a soft shade of red, the sun settling into a bank of fluffy clouds hanging just above a distant rise of mountains.

The flight had been a comfortable one with no turbulence, and the views had certainly been breathtaking, from the green, tree-lined passes to the slate-grey streams to the brown and rocky mountain tops.

The pilot and his navigator had been entertaining, also, telling stories of past adventures and boasting of the celebrities they'd transported to all areas of the West and the North Country. Nevertheless, after two hours in the small plane, all aboard were happy to feel the wheels of the plane catch the runway.

As the plane taxied toward a squat, rectangular, metal building, Beth leaned into Mike's shoulder and squeezed his hand. She could feel her heart pounding rapidly, and it brought a smile to her face because it was caused by not only the adventure they were about to embark on, but just as much by her love for this man who filled her life with so much joy.

Mike was also feeling a bit emotional, completely content and happy. He inhaled deeply and in doing so brought the essence of Euphoria that Beth was wearing fully into his nostrils. The smell made him heady. He bent his head slightly to kiss her auburn hair.

Beth looked up, a gesture rewarded by Mike's wide smile and sparkling blue eyes. "I love you, too," she whispered.

He kissed her forehead, then gave her a hug.

The engines coughed to a halt, and the pilot turned in his seat to say, "We're here. Welcome to God's Country!"

The navigator moved from his seat and walked to the door on the side of the craft. Twisting a lever, he opened the hatch and stuck his head out. "Beautiful day. Still a little sunshine left, too." He reached out to grab the hand of an attendant on the ground, then stepped from the plane shouting, "Wally, you 'ole son of a gun. How the heck are ya doing?"

Mike and Beth stood and retrieved their carry-on luggage.

Stretching his arms out to his sides, Mike twisted his back and rotated his shoulders.

Beth put down her bag and began to massage between his shoulders.

"I can stand a lot more of that," he promised.

"You'll be saying that for most of your stay," the pilot said as he walked by. "From what others have told me on the trip back, y'all will feel muscles this week you forgot you have."

Beth looked at Mike and said, "Now whose ideas was this anyway?"

Of course they both knew, though it was almost unbelievable how the trip had come about. It was only a month ago when Beth had said to Mike back in Milford, "Sexy Man, they're giving dance lessons tonight over at that new place that's just opened. Can we go?"

"What new place?"

"The Cowboy Dance Hall."

"Cowboy Dance Hall?" Mike asked surprised, "Now where'd you hear about that?"

"Advertised on Cool 101.3. It sounds like fun. Can we go?"

"Pretty Girl," he started, "I'm kind of tired tonight."

"Aw," she whined. "It's Friday night. Let's go out."

"Really, it's been a tough week. I've had to work really hard at Cool 101.3."

"Like I don't work hard at home?"

"I'm sorry. I didn't mean it like that, really. I kind of just want to stay home, maybe watch some TV or listen to that new Beatles CD."

"Come on. I'm for jumping in your Porsche Carrera 911 and going dancing."

Mike sat down on the couch and sighed, "I really am bushed. Can't we make it another time?"

Beth planted her hands on her hips. "This is exactly what Mom said you'd say."

"Whoa, that's not fair."

"Oh, come on. We don't have to stay long. I just want to see the place and watch them dance. And it wouldn't hurt us to learn some new steps." She wiggled her hips for emphasis.

"I don't really know if I'd fit in," was his response.

Frustrated, she'd said, "Oh, you. If Don wanted to go, you'd think it was a grand idea."

Right then, Mike knew that her heart was set on it. "If it means that much to you, we'll go, but we can leave when I say, OK?"

She threw her arms around him and hugged him hard. "I promise. Now go put on your dress jeans."

"Should I grab my ten-gallon hat, too?"

To which she replied, "As long as it matches my black one."

He thought she was kidding, but he found out a few minutes later that she wasn't when she stepped out of the bedroom wearing a black blouse studded with rhinestones and a black, thigh-length skirt. Her boots as well as her hat were black."

He burst out laughing. "Now what's all this?"

"Did a little shopping today," Beth stated as she spun around, a motion that caused her skirt to twirl out around her which exposed a pair of black panties. "Like it?"

A sudden rise of feeling came over Mike as he said in a hungry voice, "Yes, I like it very much."

"Good answer," she said through a sly smile. "Let's get going."

Mike took her hand as they walked out the door. For the seven years he had known this woman, she still could surprise him. He suspected the evening would be one to remember.

The line out front of the Cowboy Dance Hall looked like it could have been leading into a filming on The Nashville Network. Stetsons and leather and boots and scarves and beads and ruffles and jeans and cowboy hats were everywhere. The wait was not long, however. Once inside Mike and Beth could see why. The place was huge.

On one side was a steak-house restaurant called The Rancher. A 28-ounce Porterhouse was their touted speciality. Peanut shells on the floor and longhorn steers mounted on the walls added to the ambience. Mike and Beth approached the bar/lounge area off to the other side. Its entrance was shaped like an Old West saloon, complete with swinging, louvered doors sided with twin, gas-lit lanterns on the barn-siding walls.

Down the center of the space was a bar with stools surrounding it. Along the walls of the lower level were booths. The second level was enclosed with a waist-high railing, on top of which was a plank for drinks. Behind it were an aisle, groupings of tables, and finally another row of booths. Complete bars were built into the four corners of the upstairs.

The dance floor extended all the way around the lower bar, and hundreds of dappily-clad dancers two-stepped their way around the floor. To the back of the room were two stages, both identical in size, both emblazed with racks of lighting and decorated with banners promoting various brands of beer. On the left one, a group was performing. Soon they would alternate playing with another group on the right stage, because on the weekends there was no prerecorded music, so more than one group of musicians was employed to keep the music coming.

"Can I get you a drink?" asked a waitress dressed like a dance-hall girl.

Casting his eyes around the room, Mike saw that nearly everyone was drinking a long-necked beer. "I'll have one of those," he motioned. Beth opted for the same, and both of them moved to the side of the room to watch the action.

"I'd say this is one popular spot," Mike said into Beth's ear.

"That's what I heard."

"You said you heard about it on Cool 101.3?"

"Yeah, funny, huh? But actually, Mom said she'd heard some women talking about it."

They wandered to the back of the room, and soon the waitress came up with their drinks. "Is it true they

9

give dance lessons here?" asked Beth.

"You bet, Darling," the big-haired blonde beamed, "in the Coyote Room."

Paying her, Mike replied, "The what?"

"The Coyote Room. Over there," the server motioned with her chin. "Through that door. Walk on in."

A look of wonder came across Beth's face. "There's more?"

Tucking the money under her change cup on her tray, the girl smiled, "Sure is, Hun. There's way more."

Beth was unsure as to the scope of the complex. With a sense of uncertainty, she walked through the door and found what seemed another club, only slightly smaller. A dozen pool tables stood along one wall, a full bar stood at the back, and video games and other diversions graced the other wall. It was less crowded, and also a degree quieter. A group of people was standing to one side of the dance floor. A colorfully-dressed couple addressed the bunch.

By the time Mike and Beth had walked over to the area, they'd heard enough to know the couple were the instructors and the lesson was about to begin. The female of the duo greeted them: "You're just in time. Set down your beers and jump in line."

Beth knew that the instructors had done her a favor. There was no time for Mike to think about joining in. She rushed him to the nearest table, took a sip from her beer, and set it down. "Here we go, Sexy Man," she whispered to him, then pecked him a kiss on his cheek. She grabbed his hand and led him to the floor.

He hesitated just long enough to take a swig of his beer and place the bottle on the table alongside hers.

"Just listen up, relax, follow our directions, go with the rhythm, and let yourself go. You ready to have fun?"

the female leader yelled.

"Yeah," they all said.

"What?" the man shouted. "You can do better than that! You ready to have fun?"

An enthusiastic, "Yeah," filled the room and immediately the music and instructions started.

Mike was relieved that he'd had no time to think. Momentarily he was frozen, but then he glanced at Beth and saw her beautiful smile. He had come along tonight to please her, and when he saw her so happy, he felt all sense of apprehension leave his body. If she wanted this, he would do his best to make sure she had a good time. Immediately his right foot tripped over his left. To his surprise, the petite female instructor caught him and said, "Just don't think about it, Darlin'. Just let your body follow the music." She released him and moved on to another dancer.

Mike took her advice. He listened to the song, one by George Strait, and let his body go with the beat. Beth moved beside him, and for the next 45 minutes they walked and swayed and swirled and shuffled and hopped and slapped and clapped and front-stepped and side-stepped and back-stepped and double-stepped and down-and-out danced to the music.

Mike wiped the perspiration from his forehead and laughed out loud. He was really enjoying himself. As he twirled Beth, making her blouse ruffle and her hem rise, he knew he had done the right thing. He realized that so many times she went along with what he wanted to do. For him to do what she wanted this night was only fair, and it was turning out to be fun.

As a flush of warmth built in her body and a little-girl giggle escaped her lips, Beth felt the stress and strain of a difficult week at home drift away. Mike was being a doll to indulge her this evening, a trait she so loved in him. She made up her mind she'd make it really special for him, also. When he spun her out and brought her back, she wrapped her arm around his back and pressed her breasts into his chest, the move full of suggestion and promise. The grin on his face and the pressure of his hand on her bottom told her he got her message.

The music ended, and the male instructor said, "Y'all did great! Congratulate yourselves with a round of applause."

The clapping not only served to reward themselves but went out to the teachers as well. Both men and women who wore hats doffed them in the couple's direction.

The female said, "Now you all go on into the main room and show 'em what you learned. Just remember to relax, follow the rhythm, and have fun."

The male added, "And later, maybe we'll see you back in this room for the bronco-riding contest." He did an impersonation of a rider on a bucking horse. "From what I saw of a few of you dancing, you'll great."

Mike could swear the guy nodded his chin his way.

Beth twirled into Mike's arms and said, "I'm so proud of you. You did so good!"

"You think so?"

"I know so. Now let's go order some fresh drinks. I'm parched."

Laughing heartily at her choice of words, Mike said, "OK, pardner, let's go rustle up a brew."

The main room had gotten even more crowded, but they did find a couple of spaces along the upper railing to set their drinks while they went to the dance floor. As one tune stopped and another started, they eased on into the flow of dancers, and for the next 30 minutes put to use what they already knew and practiced what they had learned. In short, they fit right in, dancing to the music, frolicking in their adventure, falling further in love.

From song to song, they rounded the floor, and a dizzying, light-headed, swirling swell filled their minds. People smiled at them; others tipped their hats; some told them they liked their style. In short, Mike and Beth were having a great time.

Finally as one song was ending, Mike said, "I've got to sit down for a few minutes."

"That's right," Beth said playfully, "you were tired before we came."

Mike grinned and said, "And aren't you glad I found my second wind?" He placed his right hand on the small of her back to guide her from the dance floor.

She reached down with her left hand and ran it furtively up his thigh. "You better hope you find your third when I get you home," she said through a chuckle.

Back at the table, they ordered another drink and scooted their chairs close together. Bodies side by side, they caught their breath and watched the other dancers move around the floor. The scene was nearly hypnotic, the glitter and glitz, the leather fringes swaying, the skirts billowing, the bodies spinning, the lights flashing, all a variegated river of sights and sounds.

"You dance so well," Mike said to Beth. "I'm happy to be here with you."

She reached out and took his hand. "I'm happy to be anywhere with you. Thanks for coming. Really."

He squeezed her hand, which was the perfect answer.

For the next few minutes, they simply watched and listened. After they saw one couple doing an intricate step, Beth asked, "You think you could do that one?"

"Sure," Mike snickered. "Just like I could win that

bronco-busting contest."

Beth laughed.

Then, to their great surprise, the dance instructor appeared by their table and said, "I don't think that's so funny." The look of astonishment showed on their faces.

He went on, "I'm signing up people for that right now, and I think you should enter."

"You've got to be kidding," Mike responded.

"Not at all. I was watching you while you were dancing, in there and out here. You've got great hip movement. That's what it takes."

"He's got something there," offered Beth, who then smiled.

"And the first place prize is nothing to sneeze at. A trip to a dude ranch." He held out a clipboard and put a pen in Mike's hand. "Do it."

Mike looked at Beth for encouragement.

She tapped the sheet with her finger.

Of course, the rest of the evening at the Cowboy Dance Hall was stuff that would be recounted at future dinner parties. Although the dance instructor was sure it was Mike's great hip movement, Mike later said it was pure fear and a firm grip on the saddle horn. Whichever it was, Mike was the rider who lasted the longest that evening on the bucking bronco.

As others were thrown off and suffered humiliating falls into the padding beneath the machine, Mike had stayed on through the jolting and spinning and pitching of the mechanical horse. And as the winner, he and Beth won a week's stay at the Triple Z Dude Ranch.

Of course, they were excited, but no more than when they arrived home early that morning. Immediately Beth rustled Mike into the bedroom and ordered, "Come here, my sexy cowboy." She put her hands on his shoulders and pulled him toward her, planting a hot kiss on his lips. "You were incredible," she told him. "I hope you can repeat that ride."

Half-sarcastically, he said, "I don't know. I'm pretty tired."

She quickly undid the buttons on his shirt and yanked it down off his shoulders. "Well, then, find that third wind, because you've got some more riding to do." She pulled the shirt from his pants and threw it onto the floor. She leaned toward his neck, opened her mouth, and closed her lips over the skin beneath his jaw. He tasted salty; a tinge of Kouros lingering there. "Oh my," she uttered. "You are making me hotter and hotter."

"You?" he asked.

"Yeah, me," she went on, trailing her lips down over his chest and onto his stomach.

Though some men might have stood there selfishly, Mike could not help but become involved. He set his hands upon her shoulders and drew her upward which caused the brim of the hat she still wore to tip backward and fall, only to be caught by the chin strap. Gently he worked the buttons on her blouse free and moved it back, raising its tail from her skirt in the process and exposing her black bra. "That's a sight," he breathed out as he lowered his head to the V between the cups. Then he breathed in the aroma of Euphoria, and it made his head spin. Skillfully, he undid the clasp and let the bra fall. He kissed and suckled her right nipple, delicately fondling the left with his hand, then he switched to the other.

Beth cradled his head in her arm and, reaching around with her hand, clawed at his scalp through his salt and pepper hair. The actions froze them together; energy flowed from breast to mouth, from head to hand. They both shivered with the sensation.

15

Then at the same time, both of them reached with their hands downward, she for his pants, he for her skirt, undoing belts, buttons, and zippers. They breathed heavily, hungrily kissing as their legs and feet shimmied and shook to shed the material holding them back from intertwining totally.

Soon they stood tummy to tummy. A thin layer of nylon and cotton, panties and briefs was all that they wore, except for the black cowboy hat still dangling down Beth's back.

Turning his palm inward, Mike slid his hand inside the elastic band of her panties.

She inhaled to make the access easier, and quickly his hand rested over her most warm spot. He cupped her, subtly exerted pressure, slowly spread his fingers, then brought them back together again.

She nearly lost her balance as the muscles of her legs weakened to accept his advance. She exhaled a hot breath across his chest and reached down with her hand to find his strength addressing her. "Ooh," she cooed. "What have we here?"

"Your stallion ready for a ride," was his answer.

She wrapped her fingers around him and raised her head to be kissed.

He firmly planted his mouth on hers and caressed her lips with his mouth and met her tongue with his. His hand equally caressed her most sensitive part.

She offered no resistance, offering herself to him for the taking. To assist the process, she sat backward on the bed, and in doing so felt the hat bump on her back. As Mike moved toward her, erect in all his glory, she found herself overcome with a mischievous notion that she could not put from her mind. Without thinking twice, she removed the hat and set it fully onto the outstretched form

Mike was sporting. Instantaneously, she burst into laughter.

Mike saw the move coming, but did not try to prevent it. He too laughed hard as he stood there "holding" the hat. "You are so funny," he said.

She replied, "You are so talented." She snatched the hat off and flung it to the floor. Quickly she reached around Mike, grabbed his bottom, and drew him to her, kissing his stomach in the process. "You are very talented," she repeated as she felt his weight upon her, and in a matter of seconds said it a third time as he joined her totally, uniting them as only two people in love can be.

CHAPTER TWO

"Howdy, folks," the well-built man who stood about six-foot-two greeted them on the grass of the landing strip. He appeared to be in his late 50s. A thick, brown caterpillar of a mustache curled on his upper lip. Wisps of salt-and-pepper hair sprang from under his hat. He wore a black leather vest over a white shirt with a bolo tie. A silver belt buckle shone in the evening light. In its center were three Zs. "I know the pilot probably welcomed you, but let me officially welcome y'all to the Triple Z Ranch. I'm the owner, Wally West." He extended his hand "You must be Mr. Bronco-Buster himself, Mike Butts, I presume."

Mike took the rough paw that showed Wally put in his share of manual labor. "Thanks, and this is Beth, Beth Butts."

Wally shook her hand also, adding, "Pleased to meet you, ma'am."

"Beth, please," Beth said. "What a beautiful location you have." She waved her hand around, pointing to the ranch land, the stream, the mountains in the distance. "Simply beautiful."

"Why, thank you. And you haven't seen but an inch of it." He motioned for them to follow him. "Now come on, let's get you on over to the ranch so you can get settled in." He walked swiftly toward the side of the building serving as hanger and office for his airport. "Your coach awaits."

As they rounded to the front of the building, Beth was expecting to see an Explorer, a Tahoe, an Expedition, or possibly even a Hummer. But an immediate

Cinderella image popped into her head and her mouth fell open when standing in front of them was a real coach, a stage coach to be exact, complete with a team of four horses.

Wally was smiling broadly at their reaction. "Bet you expected a four-by-four, didn't 'cha? Well, we try to recapture the real Old West here at the Triple Z. Lots of dude ranches have cattle and horses and grub and pretty much authentic activities, but none that I know of take their guests up to the main house in an original stage coach. What 'cha think?"

"I'm impressed," said Mike.

"Kind of romantic," commented Beth. "Not exactly the Porsche Carrera 911, is it Sexy Man?"

"Not at all," he agreed, taking her hand.

"Well, your luggage is already on board. Not like we have to wait for the carousel to dump 'em out at baggage claim at Baltimore. Things are a bit more basic out here." He walked to the door and reached for the knob. But before he opened it, he said, "You know, we do things a bit different out here, too. I know the wife will go over some things with you at the ranch house. What she says is very nice, but let me give you my little lecture out here so you and God can hear."

A look of concern crossed their faces, which Wally noticed. "Oh, don't worry. You're gonna have a great time, but we do try to make some of this stuff authentic. You just let us know if it gets too authentic, OK?"

They nodded.

He took off his hat, which gave the moment a solemn touch. "Here goes: we try to make it fun, but this here's a real ranch for the most part, so don't expect a picnic. There's going to be some work involved, and being on the range, well there's going to be some annoyance, some discomfort, heck, there may even be a hardship or two, but we'll do our best to keep you safe, and in the end, we'll all be better people for it." He put his hat back on and said, "Well, there. How's all that sound?"

"Sounds kind of serious," Mike answered. "We were looking for a vacation. The brochure made it sound like fun, not like we'd be working on a ranch. You know we won this vacation."

"Yeah, sure, we gave it as a prize so we'd get some attention and some word of mouth, we hope. That is if you two have a good stay." He put his hat back on. "We haven't been doing this dude ranch thing for all that long." He pulled open the door to the stage and waved for them to enter. "But you're right, we've got a lot of fun things to do. It ain't all work. But let me get you up there so you can see. At the end of your stay, you'll have to let us know what you think. We're just trying to be real." He held out his hand to offer Beth assistance. He looked at Mike and said, "Beside, I figured that someone who could ride a horse like you would want to go at it full throttle. Won that bucking-bronco contest, didn't 'cha?"

"That wasn't anything," Mike started but was cut off before he could explain it really was out of the ordinary for him.

"Gotcha," Wally told him, and with a pat on the back, said, "And I got the exact right horse for you. Wait till you see 'em. Name's Thunder. Come on, let's load up so we can go get us some supper."

Once inside the coach and under way, Mike looked at Beth. "Is this what you expected?"

"Oh, don't worry about it. We aren't even at the ranch yet. It's early, sit back and relax."

"Yeah, easy for you to say. You don't have to ride Thunder."

"Silly, boy, I ride Thunder all the time. Who knows? Maybe I'll get assigned Lightning." She patted him on the leg. "This trip will be fun. Just loosen up."

She looked around the interior and spied a hand-lettered framed certificate hanging on the back wall. She scooted over to it, scanned it briefly and chuckled. "Listen here," she said, "this proves it's all meant in fun." She said, "This is called 'Hints for the Stagecoach Traveler.' It was published in the *Utah Star* in 1875. I'll read it to you: 1. The best seat inside the stagecoach is the one in the front. You'll get less bumps and jars. When any well-traveled soul offers through sympathy to exchange his back or middle seat, decline. 2. When the driver asks you to get off the coach, do it. He won't ask unless it's necessary. 3. If a team runs away, sit still. If you jump, nine times out of ten you will be hurt. 4. In cold weather, don't drink alcohol. A man will freeze twice as fast while intoxicated. 5. Don't complain about the food. Companies provide the best they can. 6. Don't keep the stage waiting. They crack the whip, and you take the trip. 7. Spit on the leeward side of the coach. 8. Don't ask how far to the next station. The driver is not a fortune teller. 9. Never handle or fire a gun while on the road. It will spook the horses and makes the passengers nervous. 10. Don't grease your hair or dust will stick in it."

She looked at Mike. "See, they put that there for two reasons. One is to say lighten up, and the other is to say things haven't changed that much over the years. Get it?"

"Well," Mike said, "I didn't hear anything about not making out in the coach when you're the only people in it. Come over here and kiss me."

Beth moved back next to him and took him up on his offer. Coming up for air, she said, "Feel better?"

"I'd feel even better if I did a little of this." He placed

his hand on her bosom.

"Then this," she put her hand in his crotch and declared, "should make you feel so good you'll forget everything."

He looked into her fun-loving, blue/green eyes and asked, "Now what was your name again?"

Placing one knee over his lap so she was straddling him, she said, "Atta boy, now you're getting into the spirit of wild, wild west." She hummed a strain from the Will Smith movie theme song.

Hurriedly Mike reached around to pull her tighter and started to undo his belt when all of a sudden the stagecoach quickly began to slow.

"Whoa, whoa there boys," they could hear Wally yelling at the team.

Beth giggled as she pecked a kiss on Mike's cheek. "Whoa, whoa there boy." She dismounted her man and said, "Better put that stallion back in the stable."

CHAPTER THREE

The ranch house was warm, friendly and very western. So was Mrs. Elisabeth West, or Bitty, as she preferred to be called. A dishwater blonde, at five feet, nine inches, she was a tall woman, and her lean body suggested she was very fit. Wearing a pair of black jeans, black, thigh-high boots, and a white cotton shirt, she came out to greet her guests and immediately put them at ease by sitting them down and offering them something to drink. "Wally," she called, "you go take their bags to the Wildcat Cabin, and I'll get them set up for dinner. We were just about to start, and they look hungry."

Bitty led them into the dining room where four other people were seated. "Say hi, everybody," she called out to them. "These folks here are just getting in. I'll let y'all introduce yourselves." That said, she excused herself to the kitchen.

"Hi," said a young, brunette woman sitting next to a dark-haired man. "I'm Suezette. This is Champ. He's my husband. We're from Alabama."

"I'm Preston," said a middle-aged, African-American male, "And this is Felicity. We're from L.A."

Beth spoke for Mike, "I'm Beth from Milford. This is Mike."

They sat down, and Beth looked around the table, and continued, "You all just get here?"

"No," said Preston. "We've been here for almost a week. I think you two are on a different schedule."

Champ spoke up, "Yeah, we're leaving tomorrow."

"We had anticipated getting in a few days ago," explained Mike, "but I had something come up at work that caused us to change the schedule."

"What's work?" asked Suezette.

"I work at Cool 101.3. Gets a little tense sometimes."

"Well, you'll forget about that here, I can assure you," she added. "Maybe even wish you were back there."

"How's that?"

"They ask you to do stuff. Not a lot of hard stuff, but chores, you know."

"Chores?" asked Beth.

"Cleaning up the stalls, grooming your horse."

"Scooping up poopie," interjected Felicity. "That's what you do in the stable."

"Ranch stuff then," surmised Mike.

"Oh, yeah, lots of ranch stuff," Champ said, "Really, I've used muscles this week that I'd forgotten I had."

"Is it that hard?" asked Beth.

"As hard as you make it, actually," commented Felicity. "I kind of took it easy compared to them. I'm not the cowgirl type, you know?" She patted her hair. "I came here mostly on account of Preston. This dude ranch thing is something he's always wanted to do."

"True. I've always wanted to be a cowboy. This was like a fantasy for me, so I really got into it," Preston explained.

Mike inquired, "So knowing how to ride is essential?"

"Oh, it helps a lot," Champ said as he took a long draw on his glass of beer. "And so does this."

"They do give you lots of instruction along with a workout," Suezette explained. "At first I thought it was kind of boring when Bart started into his lecture."

"Bart?" Mike stopped her. "I thought the owner was Wally."

"Right, Wally's the owner. Bart's in charge of the

ranch, the horses and cattle and stuff. You'll meet him in the morning, I'm sure."

Suezette continued, "And don't forget Rainbow."

"How will I ever forget Rainbow?" Felicity added, rolling her eyes.

Beth said, "Rainbow?"

"You keep your eye on her," warned Felicity in a low tone. "She's Bart's, well, girlfriend I guess. But I'm not so sure she knows that. I sure kept Preston away from her."

"Now, you be fair," Preston said in a hushed voice. "She's here to help folks learn how to ride."

Felicity leaned toward Beth. "You be sure that's all she tries to teach your man. And if she suggests a ride over to the falls, you just make sure you go along for the ride."

"Oh, hun, you're giving these nice people the wrong idea."

"Uh-uh," she said in nearly a whisper.

The tone of Preston's voice changed, but he kept the volume low when he said, "How was I supposed to know she wanted to go swimming?"

"That doesn't mean you had to oblige her."

"Baby, I didn't," he began, but she finished, "But you came back wet!"

"I told you, I fell off the horse. That make you happy for me to say it in front of everybody? Look, you all," he addressed the group, still keeping his voice just above a whisper. "Rainbow and I were chasing a stray up by the falls, we didn't find it, she said she was hot and wanted to cool off. She jumped into the pool under the falls and I fell off my horse trying to get off." He paused and clarified his answer, "Trying to dismount." He turned to his wife and said, "That make you feel better?"

"All I can say," she spoke to Beth, "is you better watch your man around that woman. She is wild."

Beth bent her head toward Felicity. "Why are you whispering?"

"Because Rainbow's Bitty's daughter."

"Oh," said Beth.

"And Bart?" Mike asked.

"Like we said, he takes care of the stables and riding and stuff," Suezette answered.

"He's the foreman," Champ explained.

"And to be really fair about it," Suezette said with a guarded giggle. "You better watch him around Beth. He has as much a wandering eye as Rainbow does."

Mike wiggled a bit in his chair. "Is that how dude ranches are?"

"Not necessarily. We've been to a couple of them," Champ said, "But I guess sometimes the cowhands get lonely, if you know what I mean."

"I've never been to a dude ranch," admitted Preston. "so I don't know. Rainbow and Bart have been nice to me, to us, now haven't they, Felicity?"

She smiled, "Yes, nice. You've just got to know where to go, as in not to the falls. And know when to say no, as in I only scooped up horse poop once."

"We'll take that to heart," Mike said.

Beth added, "And be ready to do a little work."

Champ said, "That's a good attitude. You'll get your exercise, that's for sure."

"But oh how well we feed you," piped in Bitty, who entered the room from the kitchen. This time she was accompanied by a large, American-Indian woman; they both carried huge bowls piled with food. "Family style is how we serve. So dig in, and if you don't get enough to eat, it's your own fault."

Bitty set down the food and plunked down in a chair. "I'll say grace. Bow your heads please: Our heavenly father, bless these guests in our house and bless this food. Open their eyes to see the world. Open their hearts to embrace the love that surrounds us. Open your heart to accept us all. Amen."

Chicken, strip steak, fresh trout, mashed potatoes, rice, green beans, lima beans, corn, muffins, and banana pudding for dessert - it was all placed before them on the table. Sweet tea, milk, soft drinks, and beer and wine were available to drink. Lively conversation filled the room along with the clinking of spoons against bowls, forks on plates, and ice in upturned glasses. Wally eventually joined the group. The time slipped by, and soon it was nearly nine o'clock.

Bitty spoke up, "As you old-timers know, sun-up gets here early, and for you newcomers, Beth and Mike, we start the day at daybreak, so we need to get you on to your cabin. You're probably feeling a bit tired after your trip today." With that, she stood up.

"Good night," Beth and Mike offered.

The stars were out in full, and the nearly full moon seemed close enough to touch. "Wow," Beth said as they walked along.

"Looking at the moon?" Bitty asked.

"It's so big."

"I do love it. No matter how long I've been here, each time I see that moon, it's like the first time. You ought to see it in the dead of winter, when there's snow on the ground. Makes the night look like day. I sometimes feel like I could get sunburned, well moon-burned, watching it."

"Sure is beautiful," Mike added.

Bitty walked along slowly. "I'm sure glad you like it. I like that in people. Tells me something about them."

"Like what?"

"Like they got a soul. Like they see beauty. Like they got some animal in 'em. That's what the moon's about, you know. Getting in touch with your animal side," and suddenly, with great gusto, Bitty threw her head back and let out a loud howl. When she'd finished, she suggested, "Go ahead, howl! Howl at the moon! It's good for you."

And even though at that moment it seemed silly, without having to be told again, both guests howled, loud and proud.

"Way to go," Bitty praised them.

They immediately heard yelping and baying off in the distance. Then nearby, on the other side of the house, dogs started to bark. "The animals around here are calling their welcome. Listen."

Again a chorus of howls filled the air.

Mike asked, "What are they, ranch dogs?"

Bitty stopped. "Well, we got a coupla dogs running around here. But most of that y'all hear are coyotes, maybe a fox. Probably a wolf or two."

"A wolf?" Beth said with surprise.

"Oh yeah, we got our fair share of wolves around here. But don't worry, they don't mess with us much." She waved her hand as if to send the idea off into the night. "Just like in the Three Little Pigs' book, they huff and puff and blow more than they steal the livestock."

A long, lone call filled the night air.

Turning toward the sound, Bitty said, "The full moon makes 'em all a bit crazy. Luna, lunacy, you know the connection."

The ranch dogs yipped a response.

"How many dogs do you have?" asked Mike.

"Right now? Maybe a half dozen. Sometimes they run off." She paused as if counting in her head, then said, "We got cats, too. Keeps the rodent population down. You don't hear them much unless there's a fight or there's one in heat. Cat-a-wallering. Now the wild ones, that's a different story."

"Wild?" Beth repeated the word while stepping closer to Mike.

"Oh, yeah, wildcats, like your cabin. Where'd you think we came up with the name? They're a different story." She began to walk again.

Mike asked, "How's that?"

"They aren't that afraid of us. Cougars, they can jump on a horse and take 'em down. A rider too."

"Could that happen here?" he said with a tinge of concern.

"It can. Sure. That's why our hands carry a rifle when they ride."

It was now Beth's turn to stop. "We have to carry a gun?"

Bitty faced her guests. "No, not you, not guests. Our ranch hands. It's for your protection as much as anything. But don't get focused on wild animals. We're all animals." Again she threw back her head and howled. With an air of authority, she said, "Go on, let one fly."

They did, but with a bit less enthusiasm this time.

Again a response came back through the darkness.

"See, they like you." Bitty set out again toward the cabin. "I can tell. I got a little Indian in me. It seems to come out once a month."

"And Wally?" Beth posed the question.

"Wally? Indian? Only if you count he roots for that Cleveland team. Naw, he's as Anglo-Saxon as they come. Irish-English mix, if there's a difference. Got a wild side to him though. Otherwise I wouldn't be with him."

"You two been here long?"

"Going on 30 years. Came this way via Kentucky. Wally and I met in Louisville, at the Derby. Wow, that was quite a day, but that's another story. I was a teacher. He was a seed salesman. His daddy was a farmer, and we both wanted to strike out on our own. This land deal came up, and we took it."

"How long you been doing the dude ranch thing?"

"This is our first year."

"Really?" Beth sounded surprised.

"Oh, we've had guests, but this is new to us. The cattle business is hurtin' and we are getting a little old for it. Rainbow, she's my daughter, she's got a sweet soul, but she's not going to take over a cattle ranch when we're not here. So, we did some research and took a chance that what we had here was something that people who don't have this might want to experience."

They had reached the cabin and climbed the steps.

Bitty walked inside and flipped on the light switch. Quickly, she showed them the layout. To end her little tour, she instructed them on how to turn on the jets of their private hot tub located on the patio behind the cabin.

Back at the doorway, she added, "I know Wally went over his bit about working and riding and hardships, and lots of that is true, but we do try to make you comfortable. We do ask that you help out around here, but if it's too much for you, let us know. We don't expect you to kill yourselves."

She walked out the door and stood on the other side of the threshold. "We do want you to have an unforgettable experience, and I'm sure you will. And yes, we do get up early. For you, when the sun comes up; for us, me and Wally and the ranch hands, even before that. But this is the most important thing I can tell you: We serve three meals a day, and I serve them on time, so don't be late."

"What if. . . ?" Mike began to form a question.

"Don't ask," she answered before he could finish is thought and ended their discussion by saying, "Welcome to the Triple Z. I'll see you for breakfast over at the house."

CHAPTER FOUR

The Wildcat Cabin had two bedrooms, a living area with a fireplace, over which hung a stuffed elk head, and a full kitchen which seemed useless if all meals were to be taken at the main house. "Probably left over from a former lifetime," Beth joked.

There was no phone, no television, and no alarm clock.

"No phone?" Beth said with disbelief.

Mike looked at her from across the room. "You expecting a call?"

"No big deal, I guess," Beth answered, "But I feel kind of out of touch."

"Who're you going to call? Forget about home. Things will go on just fine without you. Forget about Mom. She can get along without you for a week. Forget about Milford. People there who need to know, know where we are. They can call the main house if they need us." He hesitated for a moment like he was considering his next words and went on, "Actually, Pretty Girl, I'm very happy to have you here all to myself. I've been looking forward to it. We need this time for each other." He again paused, and when she did not respond immediately, he said, "You said you feel out of touch? Well," and a devilish grin filled his face, "I've got something for you to touch."

Beth responded to his wisecrack, "I bet you do, Sexy Man." She looked his way. She'd listened to him and appreciated what he had said. In reality, she felt the same way. Life had been very hectic lately, and they had not been as close as she would have liked. "We do need some quality time, don't we?" She walked toward him. This trip away could be just the ticket to get them back on track.

He had positioned himself next to her. "I'm going to take every advantage of having you all to myself." With that he took her into his arms and ran his hand in small circles over the small of her back.

"Oh, that feels so good," Beth moaned. "The trip here did make me a little stiff."

"Speaking of stiff. . ." Mike snickered and rubbed Beth a little lower.

"Keep rubbing, up a little higher." She, in turn, began to run her hands over his shoulder blades.

"Oh yeah, I feel what you mean." He pulled her closer, rubbing her back up and down her spine.

"You know, I am a little horny, but I also am very tired. What do you say we go check out the bed and do a little more body rubbing there?"

"And?"

"We can see what comes up," she joked, all the while kneading his muscles. "But would you be too disappointed if we waited till tomorrow? Remember, you've got some bronco busting to do."

"On Thunder."

"Right, Thunder."

"How about we jump into the shower? That'll relax us."

"And wash off some of the travel. Besides, I don't think we'll have time to shower in the morning, at least not if we want to make breakfast on time."

"That sounds good. I'll go start the water." He released her and started to walk off but stopped in the doorway to unlace his shoes.

Beth sat down on the ottoman in front of the couch

and began to remove her footwear. She glanced down at her watch and said, "What time is it here anyway? There's no clock out here, and I didn't see an alarm clock when I looked around in the bedroom."

Peeling off his socks, Mike said with puzzled look on his face. "No alarm clock? They want us on time to breakfast, but they don't provide an alarm? How are we supposed to know when to get up?" He gathered up his clothes and dropped them by the dresser in the bedroom on his way to the bathroom

She followed behind. "We know when: at the crack of dawn. We're just having a problem with how."

"I'll bet there's a rooster that crows," Mike offered as he turned on the shower, which had a doublewide stall with a bench on one side.

Beth entered the room. "Let's hope it's right outside our window." She looked into the mirror and patted her auburn hair, dirty from the trip. "Or next to the bed." She began to undress and quickly added, "And don't make any joke about the cock crowing OK?"

"You are tired," he responded.

"You're right." She lifted off her top and undid her bra, all the while thinking that he must be tired too because he hadn't taken a crack at undoing the snap himself.

Mike was already naked, leaning his bare stomach against the sink. He zipped open a small bag and brought out his shaving supplies and removed a small, plastic rectangle. "Not to worry, I brought a travel alarm." He rubbed on shaving cream.

Stepping out of her pants, Beth said, "That's good. And besides, if we're late, we can use it as an excuse: no alarm clock!" She watched him as he took the razor and worked it on his skin. No matter how many times she saw him shave, it always seemed to stir a feeling in her, the intimacy of watching a man perform his personal routine, but this was her man and his routine, and no other woman on earth was privy to this sight.

He talked as he completed his task. "So we're late. So what? What are they going to do, hang us?"

Beth stepped back and said, "I don't know. They seem kind of serious here. That might be one of their activities."

He laughed and tapped his razor on the edge of the sink. He caught some water from the tap and splashed it on his skin.

Seeing he was finished, Beth reached out and ran her nails along his biceps.

He turned from the mirror and gently placed his fingers on her soft, silky-smooth stomach. "And what are you doing?" he asked.

"Just watching, that's all. You are just so sexy."

Steam was pouring from the shower, but it wasn't the only heat in the room.

"Me? Sexy? You're kind." He trailed his fingers along the panties she still wore. "But you, you are the sexiest one." He placed his hands just above her belly button.

She gasped.

He slid his index finger inside the black material and playfully pulled the elastic band away from her skin then advanced his palm downward.

Beth moaned, and her eyes fluttered.

He moved his hand lower.

She let her body fall against his and summoning up all her energy, pushed Mike toward the shower. "Come on," she whispered, "you're steaming me up." Deftly, she removed her underwear.

They stumbled into the shower and immediately

locked into an embrace. Beth sucked on Mike's lower lip, then ran her tongue over his upper.

He met her advance by running the tip of his tongue around hers.

Their bodies were pressed against each other's. The water beat on them both. Their muscles were caught in a battle of trying to relax and being stimulated at the same time. Mike moved his mouth from her lips to her cheek to her eyes to her forehead, then he worked his way back down.

Beth offered no resistance, letting her head fall backward. Water slicked her auburn hair.

Mike ran his kisses down her neck, mixing with the spray of shower water. The hot water filled his mouth; he sucked it in and let it fall down her front. He followed its path to her breasts, taking one in his hand and the other in his mouth. Gently sucking the point, he ran a circle around her the darker area with his tongue then went back to sucking.

She drew his head closer and twisted so she was leaning against the shower wall.

Water fully hit him in the face, and he stepped back, in doing so getting a full view of her body. "You are beautiful," he said. "I love you so much." Racing though his mind was how much she amazed him. Just a few moments ago she had convinced him to put off their lovemaking. He would have gladly just held her, been happy to just have slept next to her, hear her breathing, feel her warmth, but here they were partaking of each other's pleasures once again. She had made him so excited. She was truly surprising.

He reached for the bar of soap, and ran it over her skin, starting at her shoulders, massaging the hollows above her collar bone. Slowly he worked his way over her breasts, cupping each one gingerly, cleaning under it, under her arms, running his hands down her ribcage and swinging them over her belly.

Beth pressed her back to the wall. The combination of his soapy hands and the warm water were taking her into a dream state. Her eyes rolled back into her head when he advanced below her stomach, washing her most private part with a sensual care. She relaxed ever so slightly, parting her legs just a bit, just enough for him to access the area she could hardly wait for him to touch. She emitted a slow, low sigh in appreciation of his touch.

Mike had no intention of rushing. The softness he caressed captured his complete attention, that is until he felt Beth's hand move into play, grasping him fully, giving him the attention he welcomed. He leaned against her, then put his forehead against the wall next to hers. He arched his back so they both had the space they needed to continue. The water rushing around them kept their bodies warm, but no warmer that their action.

"Oh that feels so good," he said gutturally.

"I know," she agreed.

"You are so good."

She asked, "Fast enough for you?"

His shudder was the perfect answer.

Her release followed immediately.

CHAPTER FIVE

The clanging of a dinner bell, though in this case breakfast, roused them from their sleep before the travel alarm went off. Its frenzied ringing actually occurred before the rooster crowed to wake up to his flock.

"There's your answer," Beth said groggily as she cuddled next to Mike.

"Hit the snooze alarm," was his reply.

"Funny boy." She rubbed his chest and pulled herself closer. "I went out like the proverbial light last night."

"Me too. Making love is a great tranquilizer, wouldn't you agree?"

"The way we do it, absolutely."

Mike inched toward the side of the bed.

"Come back," Beth cooed. "Just a minute. Snuggle me."

He rolled to face her, gathering her into his arms and rubbing her back. "Just a minute. I don't think we should be late."

"Why, you afraid of little itty Bitty?"

"Me, afraid?" he chuckled, "of her?" He chuckled again. "Damn right. Especially on the first day."

"Yeah, I forgot. They control the horses. Instead of Thunder, they could give you Turbo Thunder or Super Bad Thunder." She poked him in the ribs. "Or they could hang you."

"Funny girl. Come on, let's get going." He moved off the bed. "I can't wait to meet Rainbow."

She threw a pillow at him. "Well, don't forget about Bart either."

After quickly dressing in blue jeans, T-shirts, boots

and hats, they hurried from their door only to stop immediately in their tracks. The vista before them might as well have been a postcard. Seeming to stretch forever were verdant mountains preceded by a stream and an equally green valley with huge trees billowing with leaves. The sky was a deep blue with bands of orange and gold rising with the sun and mixed in with enormous patches of clouds on the horizon.

"Oh, my," Beth proclaimed, "and I thought it was beautiful last night with the stars and the full moon."

"This is incredible," Mike added. "I feel like I'm in a bubble of pure air." He inhaled. "I can't remember the last time I've smelled anything like this."

It was true. The scent of growing plants, rich soil, mountain water, ranch animals and breakfast cooking made for a concoction of aromas not often encountered in day-to-day life in Milford. "You're right. It smells so," Beth searched for the right word, "so exhilarating!"

"Good choice of words," Mike complemented her as he put his arm around her shoulder. "It does make me feel so alive."

"And it's so nice to have someone to share it with."

"I feel the same way."

Breakfast turned out to be a farewell party for the other four guests. Their luggage was set on the front porch, and they were milling around the great room when Beth and Mike walked in.

"Good morning," Champ greeted them.

"It's a beautiful morning," Beth replied. "I bet you hate to be leaving."

He nodded his head. "Yes, yes I do. But the real world awaits."

"But first," called out Bitty, "there's one more breakfast. Come in here and eat."

The group entered and faced a table aglow with candlelight. Six plates of pancakes sat in front of the chairs. Each stack had candles burning. "A simple way to say goodbye," Bitty said.

She turned to Mike and Beth and told them, "I know they all like pancakes, and I took a stab that you would, too. Anyway, we have more coming. You want to eat hearty 'cause there's lots for you to do, but I wanted to try this out as a treat for departing guests."

"A signature piece?" suggested Suezette.

"Something like that," Bitty replied.

The group all ate a robust meal, in ranch-style tradition. During it, they shared stories of the past adventures and spoke of future plans. They expressed sadness that their stay was over. They suggested they might come back. After their plates were cleared, they all went to the porch where the coach awaited.

Wally helped them aboard and climbed to his perch above the team of horses. Mike and Beth stood and waved. The horses whinnied and lunged forward. The coach lurched into motion. A cloud of dust rose after it. They were alone momentarily, but not for long, because a husky voice called their attention: "You two ready to tackle some ranch work?"

A man stood just off the edge of the porch. He tipped the brim of his black hat in their direction. His square shoulders were matched by his square jaw. Muscles bulged from beneath his long-sleeved, pale-blue work shirt. White-pearl buttons lined the front and shone from the flaps on his breast pockets and cuffs. A pair of tan, doeskin gloves were jammed in the waist band of his skin-tight, black pants. His belt buckle bore the Triple Z logo.

At first seeing him, Beth felt a slight catch in her throat. *Oh, my*, Beth said to herself, *he looks like he could be a movie star.*

Mike immediately felt the raw power of the man, a feeling he was not accustomed to acknowledging. *Oh, great*, he said to himself, *if he were smoking a cigarette, he could be the Marlboro man.*

The man lumped these two people with all the others he had met over the last year. *Oh, damn*, he said to himself, *another set of squishy, know-nothing city slickers I have to babysit for a week.*

"Bart, I take it," Mike spoke.

"Pretty smart," was the reply. "You two must be Mike Butts and Beth Butts."

Beth walked over and held out her hand, "Call me Beth, please."

He shook her hand. "Bart."

"Mike."

"Bart."

They shook hands.

"We're excited about being here." Beth offered.

Bart smiled politely. "I'll do my best to keep it that way. Lots of surprises around here."

As if on cue, a woman on a horse came trotting around from behind the building and stopped in front of them, yelling "Whoa!" in the process. A swirl of dust caught up with her and settled around them all.

"Rainbow," Mike guessed.

Bart responded, "Aren't you the smart one?"

"Hi," Rainbow shouted down at them. "I'm just in time."

From under her tan hat, which sported a braided band

emblazoned with turquoise and silver, hung long, auburn hair that trailed down over her shoulders. Her face might as well have been chiseled; her aquiline nose certainly suggested she carried her mother's Indian blood. Her brown eyes beamed with energy. Even on the horse, it was evident her legs were specimens any woman would kill for. But the feature that called out for attention most was her smile, as radiant as the sun, as polished as a gem-stone, as captivating as a crystal ball. Without even speak-ing, she could communicate simply by spreading her lips.

Upon first sight of her, Mike quickly sucked in his gut. *Oh, my*, Mike thought, *she could be a movie star*.

Beth immediately felt the sexual potency of the woman, a feeling she was not accustomed to acknowl-edging. *Oh, great*, she said to herself, *if her hair were longer, she could double as Lady Godiva*.

Bart slowly moved his head from side to side. He had seen it before, all of it. *Oh, great*, he thought, *she better be wearing a bra*.

Rainbow put her full weight on her left leg and swung her right leg over the horse to dismount. In doing so, she felt the strength of her muscles course up her perfect lower appendage. It was a sensation she enjoyed. No one ever called her a smart girl; praise usually centered on her beauty. That was OK with her, because Rainbow knew she possessed a special intelligence: she knew how to get her way, and she was not above using all her natural at-tributes to do just that. *My, my*, she said to herself eyeing the couple, *two more sheep to lead into my pasture*.

With a smile rivaling any model's magazine cover, she approached them. "Looks like we're all here. You two must be," she paused, and in the silence Bart said, "Mike Butts and Beth Butts, Mike and Beth."

"I knew that," Rainbow said with a little pout. And

she did know it. She made it a point to read over the folders on every guest who came to the Triple Z. She also knew that Bart never did that, which, she reasoned, even though he was a good foreman and was technically her fiance, did not make him a very good person to be heading up their dude ranch business. Nevertheless, he did know cattle ranching, had the ability to learn, and was great in the hay. "Welcome to the Triple Z. Have a good trip in?"

Mike spoke up, "Sure did."

"Have a good sleep?"

"Like two peas in a pod," Beth answered briskly, linking her arm through Mike's. She smiled at Rainbow.

"Well, that's what we like to hear," Rainbow said. "I know mom prides herself on making people comfortable. Now me and Bart, we pride ourselves on teaching. You two ready to get to know the ranch?"

Beth again answered. "Lead the way."

CHAPTER SIX

After a quick tour of the barn, stables and pens, Mike and Beth got their first taste of being ranch hands when they helped feed livestock and sweep out stalls. While they worked, their mentors gave them bits of information on gear and where it was kept. Mostly they left them alone after they'd issued directions, a circumstance Mike and Beth appreciated. Three other men were working the area as well, so Mike and Beth really were far from over-worked.

Whitey, the oldest of the workers, seemed the friend-liest. Probably in his late fifties and sprouting a full-faced white beard with hair to match, he spoke to them as they did their chores, "Yep, been doing this kind of work nearly all my life. Someone ought to write a book about me, I got so much experience. Been on cattle drives, cooked grub on the wide-open range, lived in a bunkhouse most of my life. The one they got here is real nice. Not as swanky as the cabins you are in, but real nice for a rough-neck to lie his tired head down in." He talked easily, tipping his head every so often like he was putting serious thought into what he was about to say. "Never been married. Al-ways had a horse. Big difference," he claimed. And he did not have to be spoken to either, for neither Beth or Mike asked him questions or urged him on. "Probably wonderin' about my name: Whitey. Don't hear much of that name nowadays. Ain't politically correct's how I think they put it."

Mike could not contain himself so he asked, "Does it have anything to do with your beard and hair?"

Whitey stopped and leaned on a pitch fork. "You're

a smart one, aren't cha? Looking at my head and this crop of whiskers I got on my face, you'd maybe come to that conclusion. Some people do. Shoot, most people do. But it ain't always been like that. Hair used to be jet black. So was the beard when I growed it. Nope, that ain't why. Reason is my first name's Francis. Don't know what my parents were thinking. No matter how you explain it on the range, that's a girl's name. Know what I mean?"

Mike nodded.

"So, my last name's White. Get the connection?"

Beth smiled.

The old man bore a big grin and said, "Sometimes life's real simple, ain't it, Darling?"

"Hey you two," Bart called, "come on over here."

Beth waved goodbye to Whitey.

Bart led them out of the stables. "Climb up here and sit," he directed as he patted the top rail of the fence that surrounded the corral. "Time you started learning."

At that moment, Rainbow walked a horse out of the stable. She held a rope in her right hand and walked on the left side of the horse. Once out of the building, she turned the horse around, closed the gate, then guided the horse through a complete turn. Immediately, Bart asked, "Did you see that?"

Mike and Beth looked at each other and then at Bart. Neither spoke.

"I take it your answer is no. That's the usual response, so don't feel bad. Actually, I expected that answer because it points out exactly what my message is going to be to you today. Observe what is happening around you. If you do that, you will learn. If you do that, you will be safe. If you do that, you will be prepared. Got that?"

They nodded.

"Fine. Now what did she do that was important? I'll

tell you. She was in control of the horse. She handled him, she turned him, she was his mind. That is what a horse wants. A horse is a smart animal. A horse has a personality. A horse wants its own way. You, however, are the leader. Do either of you have any fear of that horse?" He pointed to the animal and did not wait for their response. "If you have no fear of that animal, you're stupid. A horse can weigh up to a ton. It can kick, bite, pound you with its hooves. It can try to throw you. And that's all even if it likes you. You know why?"

He had no intention of letting them answer. "Because it's an animal that's been preyed upon for centuries. Used to be two-, maybe three-feet high at best. Big cats used to eat it. How did it defend itself? It ran. It ran at anything that looked like danger, and there were a lot of dangerous critters back then. Ever heard of a saber-toothed tiger?" He spread his fingers out and curled them for emphasis.

"And even though the horse grew, it never forgot that. For protection, horses also started traveling in herds. Safety in numbers, you know? There were dominant horses that kind of looked out for the herd. Stallions. They'd fight for superiority. They were looked up to. When they saw something that wasn't right, it was them who'd start the herd running. Can you picture that?"

Although both Beth and Mike could picture it, they didn't bother to answer. They knew Bart didn't expect them to.

"So why is all this important? Because now horses look to people to be their leaders. You must assume that role. And to do that, you have to have a healthy respect, a little bit of fear, for these powerful animals."

Through all of Bart's lecture, Rainbow stood silent. She now continued, "What we are going to show you today is what to watch for in your horse. Each horse has qualities that are caused by its history of survival of the fittest, but also each horse has its own personality. We're going to assign you a horse to work with this week and in a little while we're going to take you to that horse. But now I'm going to tell you some of the things to look for in a horse, for your protection and his.

"We don't know how much you already know about horses, but what we've found is that for even those people who have ridden horses all their lives, there's always something to learn. So, Mike, even if you're a bronco-busting master, please listen to what I'm going to tell you."

Mike could feel his face flush.

"First off, the head and hindquarters are the spots to watch. A horse's ears are crucial because they're the most mobile feature it has. Ears back? Most people think that means it's angry, but not always. If you can see the whites of its eyes when its ears are back, look out. But ears back could mean it's listening behind him, or afraid, or a little tired. When you're working with a horse, expect it to tip one or both of its ears back. That means it's paying attention. It's listening. The key is to observe so you can learn about your horse."

Beth interrupted. "Aren't these horses we'll be riding tame? Used to being ridden?"

"Yes, they are. But you're different. Each rider is different to a horse. But remember this: You're their master, and it's up to you to lead." Rainbow waited before going on. "You'll probably see most of our mounts with ears forward. That's good, a friendly position. He's alert. But one thing to look for is his ears pointed stiff and tilted to the side. That usually a sign of fear. Something is spooking him.

"As to the hindquarters, you don't ever want to be kicked, and that's a main way a horse reacts when it's threatened from the rear. So never sneak up on a horse, and when you are approaching from the back, let him know you're there. Give him a 'Whoa' or 'Easy, Fella.' And a twitching tail is nearly always bad news. It's used mostly as a threat, so stay out of the way if you see it." She looked to Bart.

He nodded. "Now Rainbow's going to show you how to harness your horse. We'll usually be around to help you with that, but if we're not and you have to catch your horse, knowing this is crucial. Go ahead, Rainbow."

The first thing she did was quickly remove the harness from the horse. She then cleared her throat and showed them the lead rope she held in her right hand.

Bart spoke, "Look how she holds that rope. No coil to it. You coil it and the horse takes off, so does your arm. She works it back and forth in her hand, kind of like a figure eight."

Rainbow held out her hand to show them. "There's lots to learn about ropes, but I'm gonna try and keep this short and sweet. Watch as I talk you through it."

The fence post was getting uncomfortable, so Mike shifted.

Bart, noticing the motion, said, "I know this might seem like a waste of time, especially for somebody who knows about horses, but it's very important."

Mike was taken aback by the response. "I was just shifting my weight around. I didn't think it wasn't important."

"Don't want to bore you," Bart said with a huff.

Mike shrugged his shoulders. "I'm not bored."

"Me neither," Beth spoke up. "Keep going, Rainbow, please."

Rainbow nodded and touched the horse on his left shoulder. She said, "Whoa, boy," and reached under his neck with her right hand, running the lead rope up and over. She then made a loop around his neck to hold him. She had the halter buckle in her left hand, the strap in her right. Moving it up his nose, she let go of the buckle, and using her left hand, placed the nose band of the halter in position. Still holding the horse with the loop around his neck, she buckled the halter and snapped the rope to the halter. Gently patting the horse on the neck, she said to Mike and Beth, "Simple, huh?"

When neither responded, Bart said, "I'm sure Mike finds this simple, so why don't we have Beth come over and try it."

As Beth walked toward the horse, Bart reached into his back pocket and tossed a pair of leather gloves to her, saying, "These should fit."

"Thanks," she said pulling them on. "They do."

"They'll make working with the horse a whole lot less painful," he promised.

Rainbow stood by the horse. "Here you go," she said to Beth, handing her the rope. "Give it a try."

Beth followed Rainbow's instruction and completed the task.

"You made it look easy," Rainbow praised her.

"Thanks," Beth said, then asked, "What's his name?"

"This guy's name is Buster."

Beth rubbed his skin just below his withers and said, "Good Boy."

"Mike, you're next," Bart directed.

Beth returned the rope to Rainbow and moved toward the fence. She winked at Mike as they passed.

"Gloves?" Mike said to Bart who threw a pair into the air in response.

Mike caught them and taking the rope from Rainbow, went through the drill. "How's that?" he asked when he was done.

"Good job," Rainbow patted him on the back.

Feeling for a second like he was the horse, Mike uttered a quick, "Thanks." It was a bit uncomfortable, so he quickly went to rubbing Buster's neck to change the focus of attention away from himself. "Good Boy, Buster," he offered.

Bart came over and took the rope. "You two catch on pretty good. Like I said, it may seem simple, but if you ever have to do it yourself, without us around, you should know how."

Beth came forward and asked, "Can I have Buster for my horse?"

"You like him, huh?" said Rainbow. "He is a sweetie, all right. But he was used all this past week, and we're gonna rest him. No, you'll have Freckles."

Beth seemed a little disappointed, but then perked up and inquired, "When will I see him?"

Bart answered, "First off, Freckles is a filly, and second, a little later today. Before you meet your horse, you got some more learnin' to do. Got to know how to lead a horse, open a gate, turn a horse, and saddle one. After that you get your mount. Follow me," he said striding toward the stable.

For the next two hours, Bart and Rainbow instructed Beth and Mike on the Triple Z Dude Ranch techniques they'd need to handle a horse safely. Both Mike and Beth gained a sense of respect for their teachers and the animals they were working with.

Bart was brusque; Rainbow was looser.

Mike and Beth did as they were told, observed, and repeated the procedures demonstrated. By the time Buster was saddled and mounted and dismounted and unsaddled, and saddled, mounted, dismounted, and unsaddled again, all four humans were ready for the clanging of the bell signaling lunch.

"Go wash the stink off your hands," Bart's directed, "then scoot on over to the big house. Bitty don't like to be kept waiting."

The tenderfoots minded.

"So you made it through the morning," Wally said through a mouthful of food.

"That's right," Beth answered. "And this afternoon we meet our mounts. I'm getting Freckles."

"A right nice filly she is, too," Wally stated. "You two will make a great match."

"I'm excited," she said. "After what Bart and Rainbow showed us, I think I'm ready."

"She did fine, Wally," Bart affirmed Beth's comment. "So'd he," Bart motioned to Mike.

Wally wiped his chin with his napkin and said, "We're real proud of our training program. Some say it's too much, especially folks like you, Mike, a rodeo type and all, but we think it's best to go over the basics. Don't 'cha agree?"

"I couldn't agree with you more," Mike began, "and about that rodeo, er that bronco riding thing--"

"Don't mention it." interrupted Wally. "I appreciate how you feel. Even I who've been riding since I can't remember when I started, even I like to see how other folk do it. Why myself, I can't wait to see you and Thunder together." He nodded his head quickly. "I bet I'll learn a thing or two from that myself."

"I've been thinking about Thunder," Mike spoke cautiously. "I don't have to ride him. I don't mind taking any other horse you have that might be rested and all."

Wally laughed. "No, no, he's all yours." He chuckled again and said, "And he's well rested. See, Thunder ain't been ridden at all."

Beth had watched the events unfold concerning Mike's riding reputation and had given him leeway to deal with the situation himself; however, she could see he wasn't handling it very well. She wondered why didn't he just speak up and tell Wally that the bronco-busting thing was happenstance? It was true, he had stayed on that mechanical horse longer than anyone else that night, and some of the men who tried were expert riders, but that had just been just luck. This was a real, live horse he'd be dealing with. Was his male ego that big? Was he willing to break his skull simply because he didn't want to speak up? She didn't care about his ego; right now, all she cared about was his safety, so she decided to intervene and said, "Wally, I don't know if it's such a good idea for Mike to ride Thunder."

Bart became her instant ally. "I agree. The horse is crazy. No one can ride him."

Mike saw his chance. "He's probably right. I'm not sure I'm ready."

But Rainbow disagreed. "Mike won't have any trouble with Thunder."

The group fell quiet.

She went on. "I caught Thunder, and I get to say who will ride him. Mike is the one."

Wally pushed himself away from the table and said, "That's my girl. Never been wrong on a rider before. Mike, you're our guy." He stood up and left the room.

Bart abruptly shoved his chair back from the table, rose, and stormed out.

Beth looked from Mike to Rainbow and back to Mike, waiting for him to speak.

He didn't.

Rainbow did. She looked searchingly into Mike's eyes. "You can ride Thunder."

"How do you know that?" demanded Beth.

"How can you ask that?" was the reply.

Beth could feel her face flush. She looked hard at Rainbow. "What makes you think you know so much about my man?"

"Beth," Rainbow said sternly, "I know horses, and I know men. This one," she motioned to Mike with her thumb, "your man, has the power. I'd think you'd know that."

"I know all about his power," Beth nearly shouted, "I just don't want him to break his neck proving something that isn't worth proving."

Rainbow inquired, "Who's to say what's worth proving?"

"I'm saying he's worth more to me than any crazy horse."

"You obviously don't know what that crazy horse is worth to me."

"It's stupid for Mike to try to ride him." She looked at Mike for support, but Rainbow derailed her plea with a direct question to him, "You can ride Thunder, can't you?"

Mike was caught, and he knew the simplest way to get out of it was to say no, but there was something in the way Rainbow spoke that gave him a dangerous level of confidence. He knew that Beth was right, but there was also something in the way she had presented her doubt. Bart had also cast aspersions to his ability. But Mike still had his wits about him; he knew riding a real horse was drastically different from that trick, metal contraption he'd ridden at the Cowboy Dance Hall. Nevertheless, he had stayed on, hadn't he? And this woman did know horses and she had complete confidence in him. Putting no more thought into it, he said, "I think I can."

Beth could hardly believe her ears. "What?" she asked incredulously.

"I think I can ride Thunder," he said again.

Beth screwed up her face and shook her head slowly, "Well, we'll just see, won't we?" Then, even though she felt like bonking him on the noggin, she did what she knew was best considering the circumstances. She put her hand on his, smiled as best she could, and said, "And I'll be cheering for you the whole time."

As they approached the corral, they could see Bart standing next to the door leading into the barn. From out of the dim interior, Whitey walked leading an Appaloosa, saddled and ready to ride. "I'll bet that's Freckles," Mike said.

"Correct," said Rainbow.

Beth said, "She's so cute," and broke into a jog toward the fence.

Before the other two could catch up, she had slipped into the yard and moved toward the horse.

"Slow up," cautioned Bart. "Remember what we told you. Let 'em see you."

She did as told and stepped toward Freckles and Whitey. "Hey, girl," she quietly spoke. "You're so pretty."

The horse perked up her ears and looked at Beth.

"She likes you," Whitey said. "Here, take her reins."

Beth eagerly took the straps. She placed her hand on Freckles' nose and gently rubbed the soft skin. "Oh, you're so nice."

By this time Mike and Rainbow had caught up.

"She's perfect for you." Rainbow told her.

Wanting to say, *So you know horses and men, and now women, too*, Beth held back the remark.

Rainbow told Beth, "Lead her around. Walk with her. Get to know her."

Silently, Beth did.

Beth took her time with the activity. It was a big corral, but when she reached the far side, she immediately wondered if it was big enough, because when she turned the filly around, she saw Whitey coming from the stable with a chestnut-brown mount that seemed none too happy to be there. Pounding its hooves, the chestnut Morgan reared up and whinnied loudly. Whitey moved to the side as Thunder crashed down and lunged forward. The rope flew from his hand and the horse raced forward, right at Mike.

"Look out," Beth shouted, which caused Freckles to lurch to the side. Beth moved with her and settled her down, all the while watching the impending collision on the other side of pen. She could see Bart smiling broadly. She could see Rainbow stepping forward. She could see Thunder's feet throwing up clumps of dirt. She could see Mike standing still, and even though she could not see his face, she knew him well enough after their seven years together to know he was gritting his jaw and was not about to move.

For Beth, the next five seconds seemed like a day. She could see every muscle in the rampant steed's chest strain as it rushed forward. She could see the nearly imperceptible motion of Mike's arm as he moved it out from his body and raised it shoulder high. His hand was open. It was not rigid like an officer's demanding a stop; it was more like a friendly gesture promising peace.

Thunder slowed and thumped to a halt, throwing dirt in the air along with bits of clay and sand that flew all about Mike like a plume of smoke. And when it cleared, Beth could see Mike standing next to Thunder, rubbing his neck, speaking into his ear. Everything was fine. Everybody was safe. Everyone was astonished, Beth included. Already Rainbow was talking to Mike. Beth felt her dander rise, but she willed an outward calm. She led Freckles across the corral and asked Whitey to take the horse. By the time she was within earshot of Mike, she heard Rainbow say, "You were God-like."

For heaven's sake, Beth said to herself, and to Mike uttered, "I see you've met Thunder."

"And lived to tell it." He exhaled. "Incredible. What a rush."

"You're OK?"

"For a while there, I was wondering." He held the reins.

Beth was happy he was still in touch with reality. "You did great. I saw it all."

"Get up on him," said Rainbow.

"Whoa," Bart spoke. "He's not ready for that." He pushed forward so he was next to Beth. "He's got to walk him first. That's the rule."

"Not now," Rainbow asserted her authority. "He's ready to ride."

Beth asked, "You sure?"

"You saw his power."

She had. Beth made a split-second decision. "Go for it," she said.

Mike looked at Bart, then Rainbow, and finally Beth. The assured look on her face made him take a step to the side of Thunder, raise his left foot to the stirrup, and step up into the saddle. He was not sure what to expect, but felt the strength of the woman he loved urging him on. When the horse reared up slightly, Mike wondered if he'd be in for the ride of his life. Instead, Thunder put his feet down and bounced forward a few feet before settling into a quick walk.

"Amazing," Rainbow said in almost a hush. "Never seen anything like it."

Bart simply put his hands on his hips and watched as Mike directed the horse around the enclosure.

Beth's smile was a bright as a beacon, and its beam drew Mike's eyes. He felt like a man who had everything, and now he was sitting on top of the world.

CHAPTER SEVEN

The trail they took started out along a gentle roll of land used as pasture for the ranch's herd of horses, about 30 total. Cattle were pastured there, also. A roadway along the outside of the rail fence, well-worn with horse traffic, was the main path leading to all parts of the ranch.

The four riders rode along slowly, Bart in the lead, then Beth, Mike and Rainbow. It was late afternoon. The ride was to be brief because for two hours Mike and Beth had worked Thunder and Freckles within the corral, a familiarization process that all riders, even the spectacular ones like Mike, had to complete. Even Rainbow agreed.

"First off, the mount." That's how Rainbow had begun the lesson. "I know you may know some or all of this, but I'm going to give you my version." She put her left foot into the stirrup and pushed upward. The muscles of her thigh tightened to spring her into the saddle. Tossing back her auburn hair, she sat upright and said, "Go ahead, get on your horses." She paused as Mike and Beth rose on their mounts, and then she instructed them, "Do as I do." She removed both feet from the stirrups. "Now sit up straight and reach your hands for the sky" She waited for them to accomplish the position. "Good, now open your legs wide but keep your knees straight. Stretch them as far away from the horse as you can." Again she paused and said, "Good. Now relax." After a moment she said, "Put your feet in the stirrups again. Do you sense how it feels? That is the seated position I want you to get in while you're in the saddle."

While Mike and Beth sat in their saddles, Rainbow continued her explanation of proper riding technique: "Horses are only as smart as their riders, so with you two, we have a head start on a great week. We're looking to make you a team, you and your mount, and although your horse has a brain, we want you to think of the team as you being the mind and the horse being the body. Though when you two learn each other, the two will mix, and that is beautiful.

"Good posture is imperative to good riding. Stand up on your stirrups." She demonstrated. "Feel your position. Gravity is flowing through your body in a straight line, from your ears through your shoulders, down your back and hips and all the way to your ankles. Now bend your knees," she followed her own instruction and watched as her students did so. "Go lower." She did. "And slowly lower. Now where are you?" As with Mike and Beth, she was seated on the saddle. "This is the position that will help you and the horse be one.

"How you and the horse perform together is dependent on balance and control. How you move your body will affect how the horse moves. If you're balanced, that's the way the horse will be, also.

"Gravity is your friend, as long as you keep your line, toes to ankles. Sitting on a horse with the legs too far forward disturbs the vertical line of gravity. If your legs are forward or backward, it's impossible to maintain balance. And remember, the horse is moving, so that is what we are going to do now. Let's walk our horses around the corral." She clicked to make her horse, Beauty, move. "Feel the gravity flowing through your body. Let your legs grow long, as though you're reaching with your heels for the ground. Feel your feet in the stirrups. Sit straight, as though your were reaching for the sky. This is the position you want. Now take a deep breath and relax your muscles."

She looked at Bart who was sitting on the fence rail. "How're they looking?"

He gave her an unenthusiastic thumbs up.

"Stirrups the right length?"

He nodded.

Rainbow looked at her pupils. "Don't relax completely. Keep your spine straight and try to just relax the lower body. Try to imagine that part of your body as part of the horse. Your upper body, including your brain, is yours. Now we're gonna practice. Let's walk."

The three of them got in a line, Rainbow at the end.

Beth, in the lead, twisted back to smile at Mike, and when she did, Rainbow yelled, "Keep looking forward!"

Beth immediately did so.

"I don't mean to be a bitch about it," Rainbow explained, "I know you two want to share this moment, but right now it's more important to share with your horse, so concentrate on joining mentally and physically with Freckles. OK, Beth?"

Keeping her eyes and body forward, Beth gave the thumbs up signal she'd seen Bart use.

Rainbow continued the instruction: "We're looking for rhythm here. Feel it? Close your eyes. Take a deep breath. Block out everything else. Concentrate on the horse, how it's moving. Feel its muscles. Listen to its hoof hit the dirt. Get into that rhythm. Try to predict when the next one will hit. And now, if you've done what I've asked, realize that even when your eyes are closed, its eyes are open. Your horse is taking care of you. Trust." She smiled even though they could not see the gesture, for she knew those words always hit home. "Now we're gonna pick up the pace a little."

The three moved a bit faster, and Rainbow said, "The faster you go, the more you'll bounce in the saddle. Your pelvis and lower back have to move to absorb the shock. Don't lock up your hip and back muscles. Allow the pelvis to rotate, to absorb, like this," she urged her horse to pass them, demonstrating the move in a rather exaggerated, and blatantly sexual manner. "Kind of like making love. I'll bet you know how to do that," she said, looking directly at Mike.

"Flatten your back," she directed Beth. "Now rotate the hips." She went through the motion again, for Mike's benefit, Beth was sure. Beth mimicked the motion.

Rainbow praised her. "You've got it." Then she added, "Opening and relaxing the buttocks will also help your body absorb the movement of the horse." Again she showed the motion. Then, looking at Mike, she said, "And, of course, we all know you've got it." She slowed Beauty to let them pass. "Let's keep this pace for a while to practice."

As they went through the lesson, Rainbow told them about how all their body parts affected the horse's movements. "Feel your reins in your hands and always remember that the reins aren't a steering wheel. Your legs steer the horse. Drop your reins to your lap," she ordered. "Drop 'em down."

The two of them let the leather straps fall.

"Put your hands on your knees."

They did.

"See, your horse stays at the same pace. If you try to control your horse solely through the reins, it's going to be a battle, and let's face it, the horse is bigger than you, so who do you think's gonna win?

"Think of that bit in his mouth like it was in yours. You want someone yanking on it? Of course not. Heavy hands on the reins are like torture to a horse, and although some people may like that kind of stuff, horses don't.

"Think of talking to your horse through the reins, like you were whispering sweet nothings to him. You know about that too, don't you Mike?"

Beth bit her tongue.

"But just like when you're talking to a woman, don't go too far with the sweet talk. Otherwise, you'll distract her, and she'll lose concentration and get off track, wondering what you're trying to say. Right Beth?"

Gambling that a look over her shoulder was called for, Beth answered, "I've never really thought about myself as a horse, but you may be right."

A smile spread across Mike's face.

Rainbow chuckled. "They say the best thing for the inside of a woman is the outside of a horse. I'm not saying I agree, but we as a gender have a lot in common with horses. That's what's gonna make this week interesting. For all of us."

The rest of the lesson went on until both Rainbow and Bart had given their students a complete overview of how a rider should connect with the horse.

In the end, Mike and Beth felt like they had learned enough to go on to the next level and were anxious get out on the open range.

The weather was warm as they walked along. The sky was blue with just a trace of high, wispy clouds. The quartet was quiet. The sound of the horses and nature were enough.

After about a quarter mile, the fence turned to the left at a 90-degree angle and stretched off over a hillside. The four riders went straight. Ahead was a line of trees growing along the banks of a wide stream. The path followed along it.

A breeze rustled the leaves all around them. A coolness seemed to rise from the stream. A gurgling of water was just noticeable.

The sunshine was crisp. Everything seemed so full of color. The greens vibrant, the browns full-bodied, the blues depthless. It was all so stunning yet so tranquil. After spending most of the morning bending and stretching with the chores and almost the full afternoon sitting in the saddle, both Beth and Mike felt their energy leaving faster than the sun.

Rainbow had specifically told them it would be a short ride, just to test out the riding skills she'd taught them, and although at the time, both Mike and Beth might have thought they could go further, now while they rode slowly along, the thought of a long soak in the hot tub back at the Wildcat Cabin seemed like nirvana. So when they heard Bart bark out that it was time to take the horses up to a trot, they almost wanted to ask why.

Instead, they audibly clicked, as they'd been instructed, inching their new friends a bit faster, absorbing the bounces as they were told. Without realizing it, they were smiling broadly. They rode on for only a few minutes, along the well-trodden path, and then when Bart turned his horse around and stopped, so did they.

"You're lookin' good," Bart called out to them. "Lookin' good."

"Very good," Rainbow added. "I think this week's gonna be fun."

"That was fun," Beth said.

"Sure was," Mike agreed.

"Well, it's getting to be time to head back," Bart said. "You want to walk 'em or run 'em?" He didn't let them respond, instead squeezed his thighs into Bullet and rolled his pelvis forward. The Arabian dug in its feet and shot off, a testament to its name.

For a second, Beth and Mike sat dazed. Then Rainbow said, "Take 'em as fast as you can back to the fence. We'll walk 'em to cool down from there." With that, she shouted "Giddy up," and was off.

They watched her race away, looked at each other briefly, then followed suit.

Freckles darted away immediately, and Beth concentrated on catching Rainbow. The two of them — woman and horse — worked as a team, moved as a unit, flowed like water down a shoot, and to her surprise, she was soon no more than five yards behind Beauty and the Bitch, a moniker she was growing fond of. But she was even more surprised when a mass of horse and man sped by her, the sound of hooves indication of why the horse Mike rode was named Thunder.

"You go, Sexy Man," she yelled over the noise of galloping horses.

Arms in front, bent at the elbows, hands gingerly holding the reins, Mike was as fluid on Thunder as smooth on silk. He waved over his shoulder as he passed Rainbow. He might have actually caught Bart if the fence had been further away. But, as instructed, he slowed to a walk when he arrived at the rails.

Rainbow was close behind.

Beth was but a few seconds more.

Rainbow pulled her horse next to Mike's and said to both of them, "Either I'm a great instructor or you two are excellent pupils."

Beth rode on the other side of Mike and Thunder and reached out her hand.

Mike took it and said, "Sometimes I feel like we can do anything."

"Sometimes we can," she replied.

Rainbow fumed. "Well I hope that includes grooming your mounts," she snipped at them.

"Not today," Bart interjected. "Whitey will do that today."

Rainbow took a defiant stand. "I think they can handle it."

"Rainbow," Bart said, as he shook his head, "you might think so, but that's not what we do on the first day." He glanced at the guests. "And as much as I'd like to agree with you, that's not what's gonna be done."

Rainbow opened her mouth, but Bart cut her off. "You made the rules. Now you live by 'em." He waved his hand at Mike and Beth, saying, "Come on, walk 'em in. Whitey's waitin' for you."

The two riders started on their way.

With a huff, Rainbow began to follow them, but Bart said, "Stay here. They know the way. You and me got some talkin' to do."

A hundred yards or so away, Mike broke the silence they had kept since leaving Bart and Rainbow. "That sounded kind of ugly."

"I suppose he'd had enough."

"Looked that way. She can get right nasty, can't she?"

Beth gave him a quizzical look. "You noticed?"

"What do you mean?"

For a split second, she thought about skirting the issue, but figured it was not fair to keep in what she was feeling. "It seems to me that she has some sort of power over you," she said, watching Mike's face for his reaction.

Dead serious, he replied, "You mean that thing with the horse, don't you?"

She had seen that look before. It was genuine. Now was the time to say what was on her mind. "That and the remarks she's been making to you and to me. That thing about sweet nothing's just about made me gag."

The horses were side by side now, at a slow walk.

Mike had picked up on the Rainbow's innuendoes but each time, he'd let them slide. He was quiet in thought for a moment, and it gave him time to reason that Rainbow's statements really didn't amount to anything. He could see how they could have been intended, how they could have been taken. He had given too much credit to Rainbow and not enough consideration to Beth. He looked at her now and said, "I'm sorry. I wasn't thinking at the time. I'm sorry if what she said hurt you."

The words caught Beth off guard. However, they reminded her that she had been hurt. "It wasn't what she said."

"I don't understand. I didn't say anything."

She nodded. "Exactly."

"But Pretty Girl, I really wasn't thinking. Or maybe it's that I was a bit intimidated. You felt that too. Like you had no right to speak. I know you did."

He was right. Their teachers included intimidation among their methods. Listen, watch, do, think. It was bossy and not the least bit receptive to input. "You're right," Beth agreed. "I didn't feel like I could ask questions or say what was on my mind."

A little smile broke across Mike's lips. "Except when you said you'd never thought of yourself as a horse. That was funny."

"You thought so?"

"I did." He nodded and chuckled remembering.

She could feel her tension lifting, but wasn't about to let him off easily. "But did you have to agree to jump on that horse just because she batted her eyes at you?"

"Oh, Pretty Girl," he began, "is that what you think?" He looked searchingly in her blue/green eyes. "That's not true. What is true is that at that moment, I did feel strong. I did. But it wasn't . . . " he stopped for a second, "it wasn't sexual, like you're putting it. I'm not crazy; I know my limitations, and at one point, I had the distinct notion to just say no, but to be honest, it had something to do with the way Bart was looking at me. Right then, and this may have played into my willingness to go on, I got caught up in showing him, and there was my pride and my wanting to make you think I was a man."

"Sexy Man, really," Beth said in disbelief. "Don't you ever think that I don't think you're a man."

"Yeah, well, you know us guys. Sometimes our egos just get in the way."

"Maybe with us girls, too," she admitted. "I didn't like her influencing you."

"I'll be honest with you," he said before he could stop himself, "a guy would have to be blind not to notice Rainbow's attractive." He saw the smile fading on Beth's face, so he continued quickly, "but influence me, she didn't. I didn't try riding Thunder because of her. It's just been frustrating, I guess, like this thing at the Cowboy Dance Hall. Hey," he said as he took off his hat and ran his hand over his salt and pepper hair, "I've been trying to explain that since I got here and nobody wants to hear it. So when she said I could do it, and really made it sound like I could, well, maybe, I was listening to only what I wanted to hear."

Beth could see that he was trying. "I was scared to

death that you'd break your neck."

"I was too, actually, but you know what really clinched it for me? I mean really sealed the deal?"

She shook her head no.

"When you said you'd be with me all the way."

"Really?"

"Really. You were what did it. And that's the way I want it."

"You know," she said, "to be honest about it, we did learn a lot today."

Mike nodded. "I did. I surprised myself."

"Me, too," Beth admitted. "But you surprised me more."

"By riding Thunder," he patted his mount gently on the neck, "my old buddy?"

"The whole riding thing."

"You did very well yourself. I'm proud of you."

"Really?" she asked. "Proud of me?"

"Yes, you gave me strength."

She leaned over and kissed the air in his direction.

They were approaching the gate to the corral. Whitey was waiting there for them. While they were still out of earshot, Mike swung his leg over and dismounted Thunder. He motioned for Beth to do the same. They both walked to the front of their horses, and he stepped closer to her and said softly, "I want to tell you right now, right here, for you and the beauty around us to hear, that it's you who matters, it's you I want to be with, it's you who influences me. If I can't please you, then nothing else matters."

A little tear formed in the corner of Beth's eye.

He saw it and touched it with his fingered glove. "Tears are welcome only if they lead to a smile."

She smiled on one side of her mouth. "I know I overreact sometimes, but I know you love me."

He returned the smile. "I do love you."

Thunder whinnied and bobbed his head.

They laughed.

"That horse does like you," Beth commented.

Mike rubbed Thunder's nose, "And he likes you, too."

CHAPTER EIGHT

"Where's Rainbow this morning?" Beth asked Bart when she and Mike walked into the barn and saw the foreman standing alone.

"Had to go off to town," he responded curtly. "You two remember what to do?"

Beth ventured, "You mean like yesterday morning?"

"No, like what you'd be doing back in Milford right about this time of day. Course that's what I meant."

"Will she be back this afternoon?" Beth asked in an attempt to diffuse the tension.

Bart snickered. "Do I look like her keeper?"

Beth could have let it drop, but she chose a direct approach, one that Felicity had advised. "I don't know who's keeping whom, but I came here to have fun. I was just being polite."

Bart's expression was hard to read, a cross between a smile and a grimace. "You're right, ma'am."

"Beth," she immediately requested.

"Beth, I've got no business taking out my frustration on you two. You're here to have fun, and it's part of my business to see that you do." He turned his head toward the back of the barn and yelled, "Whitey!"

"Yeah, Boss?" the cowpoke replied.

"Whitey, you saddle up the horses. We're goin' for a ride." He addressed Beth and Mike. "We ain't on any particular schedule now, are we? Let's say we sweep up a bit around here while Whitey fixes us up, then scoot on out and take a look at the Triple Z?"

"Great idea," Beth piped up, thinking all the while that speaking her mind was getting her further out here in the Wild West than it did back in Milford.

"Mine, too," Mike added.

"Good." Bart tossed a broom Beth's way. He motioned for Mike to follow him. They walked quickly toward the tack shop at the back of the barn. There he handed Mike a leather vest and a pair of chaps. "Try these on," he said. "We may be going through some brush today, and these'll protect you."

"How about Beth?" Mike asked.

Bart went around behind the door and came back with another set, a newer set. "I thought she might like these better."

Right away, Mike could tell Bart was right. The vest had an obvious woman's cut to it, and running down the front was a row of black, embroidered stars. "Yeah, she'll go for that. Good job, Bart."

"And these?" He held up chaps that matched the vest.

"Perfect. Did you know that her favorite color was black?"

"No. Lucky guess. Cowboy's intuition."

"What other choices did you have back there?"

Bart grinned sheepishly. "Well, let me think. I think there are a couple of others."

"And they had stars on them?"

Bart nodded his head. "Yep."

"And the stars were colored?"

"I believe all the stars were black."

Mike laughed and raised his hand in a high-five offer.

Bart obliged.

Beth came around the corner and said, "What are you boys doing back here?" Immediately she saw the vest Mike was wearing. "Hey, what's that?"

Before he had a chance to explain, Bart held out

Beth's leathers.

"For me?" she gushed, folding the soft leather into her hands and pulling it to her chest.

"Like them?"

Beth excitedly put her arms through the sleeve holes. "Like them?" she tugged on the bottom of the vest and wriggled her shoulders. "Absolutely. It's a perfect fit!"

Bart led her on. "And the stars? OK?"

"OK? They're great!"

"Mike here tells me that black is your favorite color."

"That's right."

"Then I did good, huh?"

"Yes, Bart, thank you."

"Glad to see you're having fun. Now you need me to show you how to tie on them chaps?"

"I think I know how," Beth replied. "Why don't you help Mike? He may need some assistance."

"OK, ma'am," Bart said, then immediately corrected himself. "I mean Beth."

Mike spoke up. "That's all right. I can handle it myself."

Tying the last strap onto her leg, Beth commented, "I'm sure that you can."

"Well, if'n y'all are ready," came a shout from Whitey, "these horses back here are rearin' to go."

"Well, we're rearin' to go, too," Mike spoke for the three of them. When he realized what he'd done, he looked at Bart. "Aren't we?" he asked a bit sheepishly.

"If you are, I am." He slapped Mike on the back. "Let's mount up."

"And whad'f Miss Rainbow comes back and wants to know where to rendezvous with y'all?" asked Whitey.

"Tell her she knows where she can go," Bart answered.

Before departing, Bart had to stop at the main house to pick up a packed lunch and beverages. He had them hitch their horses while he went inside.

As they waited, Mike spoke with Beth. "What did that exchange back there mean, do you think? Between Bart and Whitey."

Beth raised her eyebrows; her blue/green eyes were open wide. "Sounds like Bart and Rainbow had a fight to me."

Mike nodded. "They both seem kind of headstrong."

"That's an understatement," she said. "But maybe out here in the middle of nowhere, that's not such a bad character trait to have."

"You could be right. Personally, I would rather follow someone who takes charge than someone who's wishy-washy."

It was Beth's turn to nod. "Bart," she began, then paused. "Bart, I don't know about him. He seems like he could be mean."

"I see that, too," Mike said, "but he also seems very competent. Maybe he's just forceful. Forthright."

"He seems to struggle with his patience."

"You mean when Rainbow is around?"

Beth looked to see if Bart might be coming, then answered, "Exactly, like he wants to be in control but knows he can't go but so far."

"Or correct her if he doesn't agree with what she's doing."

"Yes."

Mike offered an explanation: "Maybe that's because it's Daddy's ranch that he works on."

"You mean Rainbow's Ranch?"

"Exactly. But I get the feeling that he knows his stuff. I'm guessing that you don't get to be ranch foreman unless you're good."

Beth stirred when she heard footsteps approaching. "I suppose we'll find out," she answered in a low voice, then spoke louder to Bart as he appeared from inside the house, "We all set?"

"Bitty fixed us up good," he beamed. "Lookie here." He peered into one of the bags and reeled off the contents, "Sandwiches, cheese, fruit." He handed it to Mike and said, "put that into your saddle bag." He opened another bag. "Cookies and muffins." He gave the bag to Beth. "And here's your canteens." He held out the water containers and showed them how to fix them on their saddles.

"And this," Bart held up a wine skin, "I'll take command of. Bitty's been real nice to us today. She makes a little red wine from the grapes she grows up on the hillside. It's nothing real fancy, no Korbel or Kendall-Jackson, but it tastes real good after an open-air lunch."

Beth spoke up, "Should we be drinking if we're riding?"

"First off," Bart responded, "we won't be on our horses for lunch." He waited for a laugh, but did not get one, so continued. "And what we got in this skin ain't gonna make all three of us drunk, if that's your concern." He thought about it a minute and added, "And if you don't want any, that's fine. We got water, too."

He mounted Bullet, shifted his weight around in the saddle and patted the wooden butt of his rifle, checking to make sure it was there.

The action was almost unnoticeable, but Mike caught it. "You really need that rifle, Bart?"

Bart guided Bullet's reins so the horse turned toward the trail. "You never know what we might run into. This is still the Wild West though there ain't as much of it as there once was," he replied. He winked and then addressed Bullet. "Giddy up."

The horse followed the direction.

So did Mike and Beth.

The mid-morning sun flowed over them like gentle ocean waves, warming their skin, soothing their minds. The three riders moved at an even pace. The trail was the same as the day before, along the fence, to the stream, following next to the trees. None of them spoke. Instead, they let nature and their thoughts intermix like swirling water, carrying them on a calm journey. They went beyond the trees and onto a flat plain that rolled out till it touched the foothills at the mountains' edge.

Bart slowed their speed. The horses began to walk. The clip-clop, clip-clop, clip-clop that filled the air was almost hypnotizing. There they were, six creatures, three of which were human, all but dots on the surface of a plain that reached back into antiquity. The long grasses swished and swayed in the balmy breeze. There was no telling if dinosaurs might have roamed the same land, if lava might have covered it, if mastodons might have lumbered on it, if glaciers might have buried it, if Indians might have crossed it, if fires might have ravaged it, if wagon trains may have rambled over it, if floods might have inundated it, if cowboys might have ridden it rounding up herds to march to market. Although it was likely that all those things had occurred, on this glorious day, all it was was a piece of wild paradise for them to behold and become part of, adding to its history.

Bart had been here before, had seen the undulating

roll of the land, the expansive patches of brush and brambles, the meandering of the stream, the flurry of quail and scurrying of rabbits. He knew all too well the location of washouts and ruts carved by cloudbursts, the danger of gopher holes, ant hills, downed logs, the possibility of coyotes, snakes, wolves, and even cougars spooking or even attacking the horses. So, unlike his uninitiated charges, Bart was cognizant of the hazards of riding the open range.

However, on a day like today, he also fell prey to the lure of the lush world around him just like the novices did. Even his thoughts could wander, and on a day like today, especially after a night like last night when he and Rainbow had gone toe-to-toe and jaw-to-jaw arguing, he let down his guard and put his faith in what he trusted impeccably, Bullet.

For a second, Bart sat up straight and keenly listened to see if his guests were talking. Sensing that they were not, he went into himself, thinking about himself and Rainbow.

Why do we get into fights like this? Why's she so stubborn and hell-bent on having her own way? The answer flashed into his mind. *Her father. He's always given her what she wants. I like Wally, like him a lot. A fine rancher, rider, but he hired me to head up this dude-ranch thing. Ever since she's got interested, it's been a pain.* Then he delved deeper and wrestled with another angle. *She's a wild one, and I shoulda never slept with her. Never shoulda. Bad for my job. Bad for my head. But that hair, those eyes, that body. When she offered, I just couldn't refuse. What man could?* And that took him another direction, one that made his blood pressure rise. *And now when she looks at a man, I get this feeling like she's lookin' at him like she first looked at me.* He could feel his fist clench. He shook his head to try to clear the feeling from his mind.

Clip-clop, clip-clop, clip-clop. The even beat of the hooves padded the ground. Beth was next in the queue, and she too was feeling the effects of the metronomic rhythm. Her thoughts came free and easy. *The air here is so clean, so crisp, even on this warm day, even as we kick up a little dust. Even that has a sweetness to it, like it's filled with life, like the earth is sending up a bouquet of creation, like it must have smelled for centuries here when creatures passed. So different than* Milford.

She looked off to the mountains in the distance. She looked to the stream and its accompanying flank of green treetops zig-zagging till they disappeared in the expanse of nature around them. She wondered where the stream led, what river it joined, what cities were downstream?

A slight gust of wind moved across her face, cooled her skin. She noticed how her auburn hair felt tucked under her hat, the perspiration gathering in the band, the subtle mixture of fresh air, sun, sweat and Euphoria that rose from her body. It was as though someone had found the dial that controlled how sensitive her senses were and had turned it up all the way.

For a moment she held her breath to hear as much as she could. The sound of insects, the stream, birds, the wind, the horses, their leather tack rubbing, their breathing, their tails swishing, and finally, she heard her own heart beating, softly, calmly, emitting not only a sound but a feeling of well-being that she accepted as a gift.

Ahead of her was the man in black, Bart, and Beth wondered how appropriate that was. He oozed western masculinity, form the way his body sat in the saddle, to the way he treated his horse. Bullet, now there was a name only a man could come up with. Fast, round, short and straight to the target, not a pairing of words most women found endearing. She reached down and touched her chaps, then the vest he had given her, complete with black stars. *He comes off as so harsh, so rough, so 'I'm so in control.' So many women fantasize about cowboys, is that what they're looking for? And then he goes and does something sweet like getting these clothes for me. Is he complex or just so simple he seems complex?* She thought of Rainbow with him. *How had they met? What was their relationship really like? What did they talk about yesterday? How did they make love?*

At that moment, Bart reached up with his right hand and scratched at his neck, in doing so, he flexed his arm muscles. The triceps and biceps made his black shirt bulge. Beth thought, *He is a piece of work. I bet he's great in bed.* And as she watched him ride, she followed the roll of his shoulders down to his back, into his hips and further to his legs, and the longer she watched, the more she could feel he was every bit as much an animal as the steed he rode. In fact, from the way his body matched Bullet's every motion, they might be one. *Did Rainbow find that attractive in him, or disdainful? A man and his horse, or a man and his woman, how much had the Old West changed?*

A strange sensation came over Beth, and she switched her attention to her own body, its posture, its movement, its juncture with Freckles, its contact with the saddle. Her thighs shifted slightly up and back, contracted to hug the saddle, then released. It was all so fluid, and she was excited to be part of something so big. A feeling of warmth came over her, and she took a long, deep breath in, only to let it out and feel more a part of the world than she could remember in a long time.

She gazed at their hands, then below them to her

legs, all sitting upon a majestic creature. It was as though she could see her skeleton and muscles working together with her horse's. And she judged that although theirs was not as masterful as was Bart and Bullet's, hers and Freckle's ride was an example of teamwork. She felt very satisfied with herself.

Sweat ran down Mike's face. Dust gathered on his skin. He took his handkerchief and wiped it away. Being last was not normally a position Mike, or Thunder for that matter, liked being in, but with the beauty of the landscape and the delightful events that had unfolded through the course of the day, it was good enough for them both. As a team, they were meshing perfectly.

Mike felt like he was part of the horse, and regardless of how he had happened to win the contest back at the Cowboy Dance Hall, and for whatever reason this spirited animal had taken a liking to him, he was not into questioning why. He was just happy to be on this fine day.

For the last hour or so, like the others, he had been caught up in reflection. Now, with his blue eyes looking straight ahead, he fully realized what his life was all about. It was not about Cool 101.3 and the degree of satisfaction he took from there. He did find solace in knowing he was productive, but there was more. He knew it was not about Don, and the degree of fraternity they shared. He did enjoy his friend and the good times they had, but there was more. He knew it was not about things, material possessions, objects like the Porsche Carrera 911 he drove. Though he appreciated the workings of a fine piece of machinery and liked the feeling of ownership, he knew there was more.

The sight of Beth in front of him brought fully to mind that there was more. *What a woman she is. She's*

79

the right woman for me. The image of Rainbow crossed his mind, and he contemplated their contact of the last few days. *The woman had power, that was undeniable, but so did* Beth. Beth *had the power to lift him up when he was sad, to lift him higher when he was happy. To make him laugh. To make him think. To make him feel secure. To make him feel wanted, needed, appreciated. She had the power to soothe him when he was riled, to move him with her words, to woo him like no one else. Never forget that,* he said to himself.

The trio moved leisurely across the field.

Mike watched and thought. *What do I give her?* That the question came to him was as much a surprise as the question itself, because like most men, Mike was more of a doer than a wonderer. *I give her happiness,* he thought first. *I protect her. I make her laugh. I stand by her when she's sad, and when she's happy. I buy her stuff.* And then he shook his head. Somehow, he was beginning to feel like she gave him more than he gave her. *That can't be true. I'm there for her. I lift her up. I show her that I love her. However,* then he stopped. *But do I do it enough?*

Mike watched Beth riding in front of him. The slight bend of her neck, the sway of her back, the rock of her hips. She was so beautiful, so sexy. If they were alone, he'd surely make a play to get them to stop and make love. And in a split second, he thought to himself, *Is that what she would want?* She was such a sexy woman; she was even sexier to him now than that seven years ago when they'd become a couple. But would she want me to be aggressive now?

His next thought shocked him in some ways, for right then an image of Rainbow popped into his brain. *Would she want it?* Mike looked up at Bart, Rainbow's lover, her stud. *I'll bet they are wild together. Cowboy, cowgirl.*

Wild West. Horses. Leather. His mind was abuzz till he came to his senses and said softly, aloud to himself, "Beth and I are too!" For proof, he thought back to last night.

Behind the Wildcat Cabin with access through the bedroom was a private, enclosed area. An eight-foot-high redwood fence held two sides. The third was made of stone, and covering three quarters of it was a waterfall leading into an oval pond. A rust-colored, terrazzo tile floor was laid throughout, and the hot tub sat in the center of the enclosure. A shower head stood in one corner. A pair of lounge chairs sat in the other.

The first night they had gotten in too late and were too tired to take advantage of the facility. On the second night, they were tired and sore, but Mike offered as an argument, "The hot water will do us good."

Beth bought it, and soon they were striped and standing under the shower. Night had settled in; only candles lit the area. Ever so quietly, Mike began to hum their favorite Beatles tune.

"You are such a romantic," she said.

"Only because you inspire me," he answered.

They stood, Mike's front to Beth's back, facing the stream of water showering down on them. He wrapped his arms around her, holding her just beneath her breasts.

She leaned her head back on his shoulder, her auburn hair against him. The warm water hit her just below her chin, ran down her neck, rushed over her chest and flowed over his hands.

He turned his palms up and caught it, then pulled it up and over her cleavage. In the process, his wrists swept over her nipples. He repeated the motion again and again.

Beth's nipples tightened with each pass until they ached for a firmer touch. She brought her hands up to his and guided them to still her need.

He applied a gentle pressure and whispered, "That feel good, Pretty Girl?"

"Yes, it does. Sexy Man." She pulled his hands tighter.

He increased his hold, sliding his right hand down so he could take her nipple fully between his index finger and thumb. He moved his fingers back and forth.

Beth emitted a slow, low moan, in doing so, turning her head so her lips were against his neck. She placed her mouth on his skin there and softly sucked. She could feel him shiver. She could also feel a reaction further down, a reaction she knew meant he was enjoying himself.

"Oh, that feels good." He pulled his body even closer to hers.

"For me, too," she replied.

"Feeling a little less tired?"

"And a little less sore."

He turned her around and planted a kiss on her lips.

She met his advance with gusto, kissing him back fully, grinding her hips into his and raking his lower back with her nails. When he tried to break away, she grabbed him and would not let him move. She did not speak; her hips were doing her talking. She ran her left hand up his side and placed it on his shoulder blade. There she pulled down, a signal he took to move his hand to her hip, which he squeezed.

"Uh-huh, yes," she cooed.

He shifted his body slightly.

She raised her right leg and wrapped it behind his thigh. "No, no. Don't move," she directed as she rubbed against him. "I'm feeling less sore all the time."

"Well, I'm feeling very stiff," he joked.

"I know, Sexy Man." She looked up at him. "I think you need a massage." Before he could answer, she reached down and took him full in her hand.

He sucked in his breath.

"You like that?" she asked.

He wasted no time thinking about words. "Yes."

Slowly Beth backed away, he still in her control. "Good. Now come with me." She inched further back. "Come with me," she told him.

In the seven years that they had been together, Mike had learned that when Beth was in this mood, to just go with it. So, as she backed up, he followed. He knew he was in good hands.

She made her way to the side of the hot tub and stopped. She looked into his blue eyes and said, "You my cowboy?"

"Your cowboy, your Sexy Man, your anything you want me to be." He could feel his heart pounding.

Beth looked up at the moon, now full in the sky.

He followed her head's motion.

"Feel like howling now?" she asked.

The sound that came out of his mouth as he threw his head back and bellowed was his answer.

"Atta boy," she praised. Then she mirrored his howl, drawing their bodies closer in the process. She held the position, then whispered, "Ooooh, you're making me sooooo hot."

"Ha," he chuckled, "and that would make me boiling. Pretty Girl, you never cease to amaze me."

"And I want to keep it that way." Still holding him in her hand, she let her body go lower, kissing him slowly and deliberately as she slid down past his neck, his chest, his stomach. What she held in her hand she saved for last.

Mike's mind felt like it was going to explode. An hour ago, he would have been satisfied with a quick shower and going to bed. Now here he was about to explode. His legs were getting rubbery. He wasn't sure he could maintain his stance. Putting his fingers on her head, he let out a guttural sound and ran his digits through her auburn hair. "Oh, Pretty Girl," he murmured.

"What? You like this?" she murmured in reply.

Once again he went with brevity. "Yes."

"Ummm, me too, my bronco-busting man." She quickly stood up and put one leg over the side of the hot tub. "And I think you'll like this, too." She released her grip and completed her entry into the water. "Come on, don't make me wait."

"Owwwwwlllll," he called to the moon and jumped into the tub.

In the distance, the yell was answered by a lone canine.

Beth hit and switch to start the jets. Bubbles danced and burst on the surface. She slide close to Mike.

He shifted his body so his back was submerged and tucked against her front.

She grabbed him with both of her arms and cradled him, saying, "How's my baby doing now?"

The water felt wonderful. Whatever aches and pains the day at the ranch had caused, they were not evident now. He floated in her arms, let his head relax in the small of her elbow, allowed all his muscles to go loose, except one, which was poking out of the water.

"I see I've still got your attention," she said.

"Full and hardy." He looked across the surface of the water. "You want me to do my hat rack impression again?"

"No, I've got something else in mind." She twisted him suddenly so his body was front down, scooted her body so she was directly underneath him, and welcomed him totally. Their union was exact.

They moved like they were made for each other, like

they were ying and yang, gin and tonic, bread and butter, horse and rider. The water whooshed around them, ran between the scant spaces between their bodies, buoyed them so they felt weightless, rushed them toward closure, and at that time, Beth tensed her body and signaled her release with a rousing, "Owwwwwlllll."

Mike matched her sound.

So did a variety of creatures in the night.

CHAPTER NINE

"Well, will ya lookie there!" Bart's baritone voice snatched Mike from his reverie. Looking forward, he saw the foreman point up to the sky and cast his gaze upward. There flying a lazy circle was an immense black-and-white bird.

"American bald eagle," Bart said. "Ain't she pretty?" He stopped Bullet, and they knew instinctively to do the same with their horses.

"Oooh," offered Beth as she watched the raptor glide along. "See him, Mike?"

"Uh-huh. What a sight. How big you think he is, Bart?"

"Wing span about eight feet I'd say." He let them marvel at the sight, then asked, "Now I know Benjamin Franklin was some kind of genius, but can you believe he wanted to make the turkey the American bird?"

Mike replied, "For a man who invented bifocals and discovered electricity, he sure did miss the boat on this one."

"What was he thinking?" Beth said. "You think he ever saw an eagle in flight?"

"Yeah, but remember he was a politician. Probably had some turkey lobbyist offering him free dinners for a year or something like that."

"That's funny," Mike complemented Bart.

"Thanks, I'm no stand-up or anything, but I get a good one off every once and a while. Lots of time to think on the range, you know?"

After their pensive morning ride, they understood completely.

Bart continued, "It makes my blood boil when I think about poachers killing an eagle for its feathers."

"What?" Mike asked.

"Oh, yeah. Eagle feathers are quite the collector's item, quite a high-ticket item. Used to be that the American Indians wore them as a sign of manhood, of invincibility, strength. Had to climb to an eagle's nest to get one; didn't kill the bird. Eagles were sacred. Still are to the Indians. And to the government, too, really."

Beth asked, "How's that?"

Bart looked over one shoulder then the other, finally focusing on Beth. "It's a Federal crime to kill an eagle. It's also against the law to possess an eagle feather."

"Really?" she said,

"Yep. That's why collectors want 'em, because it's against the law to have one. Doesn't that make sense?"

"Sure does," replied Mike. "Tell someone he can't have something, and he wants it. That's the way it always is."

"That's the way it works everywhere," Bart said. Then he sat up tall in his saddle. "OK, we've been taking our time up till now, so what say we pick it up a little? I got a place I want to get to for lunch. Just up the way. Y'all ready?"

"I'm good." Mike straightened in his saddle.

Beth readied herself. "Me, too."

"Great, follow me." Bart rocked his hips forward and clamped his thighs against Bullet. "Giddy up!"

"Go, Thunder," ordered Mike.

Beth followed suit.

The three of them went from a cantor to a gallop in a matter of seconds, leaving a trail of red dust behind them. They rode side by side, Beth, Bart, and Mike, separated by a distance of five or so yards between them. It was not a race. Bart set the pace and the others kept up. The skills they had been taught were paying off. The horses ran on almost gleefully. Their riders felt the same.

Bart looked right and shouted to Mike, "Way to go. Relax your hands more." He demonstrated. "Put more into your hips."

He looked to his left and yelled, "You are looking good!" He smiled broadly and winked, "Really good, Beth."

Beth felt a surge of energy.

The grassland moved under their feet quickly. The foothills came up fast. Wind in their faces, massive muscle rushing them to their destination, the trio soaked up the feeling.

Their route was slightly uphill. The mountainside loomed near. The vegetation was beginning to change to less grass and more scrub brush. Soon they came upon two rows of rocks jutting upward. A stream ran through a break between them. Behind them, the land rose into a forest of huge pine trees.

Bart slowed the pace until they were walking. He said, "See those rocks, the ones that look like jagged teeth sticking from the ground?" He pointed in the direction.

"They do look like a set of teeth," Beth said.

After Mike had checked out the formation, he said, "The inside ones look like fangs."

"Correct!" Bart stated. "We call this spot Cougar Point. Can you guess why?"

"Because they look like the fangs of a cougar?"

"Correct. And another reason is we got cougar around here. Lose a coupla cattle to 'em each year. Mostly they prey on deer, but once in awhile they get a taste for beef. A cat can weight 160 pounds, but I swear I've seen one in the forest up a ways that goes over 200."

"So you've seen one?"

Bart patted the butt of his rifle. "Oh, yeah." He smiled and bobbed his head, then said, "But not to worry. I've got us covered. Besides, they don't usually bother people."

"Usually?" Beth repeated his words.

"Like I said, don't worry about it, much." He twisted his body so he was facing the pines. "We need to go on a ways. Up this trail."

They were traveling over a well-worn path.

"It leads up there." He pointed to an area between two hillsides. The stream divided them making a small valley that bent around and out of sight. "It's not far. We'll have to go in single file from now on. I'll lead." He moved out in front.

Mike and Beth, of course, followed.

The scenery was now dominated by trees, rocks, and the stream. After stopping for a few minutes to let the horses have a drink, they clopped up a relatively easy trail that had woods on both sides. Then they came onto a clearing, and Bart stopped Bullet and said, "Take a gander at this."

Off to their right was a view of the flatland they'd just crossed. It stretched off as far as they could see.

"Wow," Beth said.

"Pretty, huh?" Bart said. "You can see all the way back to the ranch house if you crane your neck." He pointed off to the left. "See the smoke rising?" A slender spiral of white swirled into the air.

"Just barely," Mike replied.

"They call this spot Indian Lookout."

"I can see why," Beth said.

Bart stood up in his stirrups and held his hands over his eyes, scouting the area below. "Well, nobody's followin' us, so let's move on up."

Who would be following us? Beth and Mike both thought at the same time. They exchanged a look.

The three rode slowly into the trees and soon came to a narrower trail that immediately turned to the left which set it right against the stream, only now the water was about 30 yards below them. The dropoff was not completely vertical, but a jagged slope of broken rocks and scraggly trees was a formidable boundary that made all the riders careful to stay on the graveled path. A little further up, the way curved right, and it was here that they crossed over the flat stream, a bed of rock underfoot. Not more than ten feet away, the cool, clear water fell over an edge which created a waterfall that cascaded over a series of rocky ledges till it gathered in a wide pool only to become the stream they'd been following.

Mike dared to look downward. "Hey, a swimming hole," he yelled.

"Right," Bart replied. "But you can't get to it easily. You feel like a swim?"

Although it was cool in the shade under the trees, the air temperature was still warm. Mike ran a hand over his neck and said, "Might feel nice."

"Keep that in mind," Bart told him.

Once past the stream, the trail widened a bit but rose sharply which caused the horses to slow. "Lean into it," Bart suggested. "We'll be there soon."

Right at that moment, Freckles slipped on some pebbles, but immediately caught her footing. Beth shrieked in surprise.

"You OK?" Bart shouted.

"Well, yes," Beth answered. "It startled me."

Bart acted like it was no big deal. "Yep, it happens. But you kept your mount. Right?"

Beth nodded, still a little shaken.

Bart went on, "That's what matters. You got a natural feel for riding. I can see it. Rainbow was right about Mike, but I had a feeling about you, also."

Beth asked, "What did Rainbow say?"

"Oh, nothing," he began, "you know what she said. How he had a natural seat for riding, how he was made for riding. And how you needed some work. But after I saw how you handled Freckles, I knew you had it."

"And me?" Mike wanted to know.

"You've got it, too. Like I said, Rainbow was right." Their progress had taken them to a much flatter stretch. With his heel, Bart nudged Bullet, and in doing so said, "Now come on, we can speed this up."

Mike looked at Beth, and they both went after Bart.

Momentarily, they went down a little incline. Immediately in front of them was a sapphire-blue lake. Built along a sandy cove was a log cabin with a porch, a small corral with an attached shed, and a dock with a canoe at its end. "This here's our mountain lodge," he boasted. "We're gonna have lunch here. What'cha think?"

"Looks like the perfect getaway," Beth said.

"Are we going swimming?" asked Mike.

"Anything you want," Bart replied.

Oh, don't encourage him, Beth thought, wondering just how cold that water was.

Bart dismounted and ran his hand over Bullet's nose. "There, boy, you're the best, aren't you? Aren't you a good boy? Yes, you are." He spoke in an uncharacteristic sing-song voice. "Yes, you are."

Mike and Beth got off their mounts as well, but did not lavish praise over their horses even though they felt like they deserved it. Once on the ground, Mike noticed how rubbery his legs were, and with a knowing smile on his face thought how similar the feeling was to the one he'd had the night before in the hot tub.

"Finding your land legs?" Bart asked.

"Sort of," Mike answered. "Funny how you don't think about how much your body's working while you're riding. At least not till you stop."

"You, too?" Beth commented. "I was wondering if it was just me."

Bart pulled a pocket watch from his jeans' pocket. "We been riding for about an hour and a half. That's a good workout."

"Come to think of it," Beth said, "I've worked up quite an appetite, too."

"Yep, fresh air'll do that to you." Bart took Bullet's reins and began to lead him toward the corral. "Let's get these guys in the pen, and we'll eat."

Once they'd cared for the horses, they took their lunch to the cabin's porch and set it down and sat down on the wooden planking. "This old place was built by the original owner way back before Wally and Bitty bought the ranch. Supposedly the foundation is built with rocks that came from the mine he was prospecting."

The three riders began to take the food out of the saddle bags. "A gold mine?" Mike asked.

"That's the story, but there's never been enough gold in these parts to shake a stick at, according to the old-timers still about. They say the geezer who came out here to look for gold was a dreamer. Everybody knows this land's made to ranch, not mine. After no gold was found, this cabin was used, well it still is really, by ranch hands working the upper pasture. We still got cattle there. I'm going up a little later to check on 'em. It makes for a great overnight or for when branding time comes."

"We're going up further?" Mike asked.

"No, I'm going to do that. Got to check a fence. See

if the herd is OK. You two're gonna stay here and catch some rest."

Beth asked, "What are we going to do here?"

Bart handed out the sandwiches. "Anything you want. Use your imagination. Just don't head out on horseback without me. I'll only be a coupla hours max." He offered them a drink from the wine sack.

"Well, since we aren't driving." Mike took the leather pouch and squirted the wine toward his mouth. It went wide and hit him in the cheek.

"Don't know where your mouth is?" kidded Bart, who took the sack and demonstrated the proper procedure. "Ahh," he uttered after swallowing. "That Bitty makes a good red wine." He passed it over to Beth.

She took her turn, perfectly placing the stream of red liquid between her lips.

"Bravo, senorita," Bart lauded her. "Bravo."

They ate and talked and drank, all the while basking in the warm sun and rich mountain air. After about 40 minutes, Bart stood and said, "Well, I'd like to take a nap, but I've got to tend that fence. There's a trail around the lake if you feel like a walk. There's bunks in the cabin if you feel like a nap, or whatever," he threw in. "And, of course, there's the lake. So, Mike, if you really want to take a swim, have at it."

"That's OK," Mike replied. "I forgot my suit."

"No problem," Bart said with a sense of satisfaction, "we got suits." He led them into the cabin and pointed to a rack of clothes on the wall. "Here's some swimwear right here. Help yourself. It ain't Calvin Klein or Hilfiger or anything fancy like that, but I believe we got a coupla sizes and styles to choose from." He backed away to let them look, then added, "Of course, if you're partial to your birthday suits, that works around here right fine. It's up to you."

Beth reached out to touch a one-piece black suit. "I think we'll find something to use out of this, thanks."

"No problem. I'm sure you'll enjoy yourselves. There are towels over in that dresser. Bitty keeps 'em fresh for times like these."

"That Bitty is quite a gal, isn't she?" Mike said.

"There's none finer." Bart moved to the door, but before going over the threshold, he stopped to say, "Oh, and a few things before I get out of here. Your horses'll be fine. I'll check on 'em before I leave. And if you do go for that walk, don't go too far off the trail, OK?"

"Why?" Beth wanted to know.

"Well, you remember Cougar Point we rode by?"

She nodded.

"Not to mention the bears or the wolves."

"What?" Mike tried to lighten the mood with a Wizard of Oz reference. "No lions and tiger, oh my?"

"Cougars are like tigers," Bart responded.

"I get it," Mike stated. "Stay on the trail."

"And if you hear some rustling in the bushes," Bart began to say, but Beth cut him off, saying, "It better not be you."

He laughed. "Fair enough. I'll give you a big ole holler when I get close." He turned to leave.

"Bart," Mike stopped him. "I know this won't happen, but what if for some reason you don't come back?"

Bart smiled. "Good question. Two choices. You know the way home, go on back. Or you could spend the night and wait for me. But above all else, don't come looking for me. I don't need you lost out here. Got that?"

"Got it."

Bart raised his hand to the brim of his hat, dipped it down to say goodbye, and quickly walked away.

Standing in the dimly-lit cabin, Mike and Beth looked at each other, looked around the interior, then looked back at each other. "So here we are in the Wild West," he said.

"Lions and tigers and bears, oh my!" offered Beth, which didn't exactly come off as light-hearted.

"As long as those flying monkeys don't show up," Mike replied.

"How about the Wicked Witch of the West?"

"Rainbow?"

The quick comeback made Beth laugh. "Her, too. What do you suppose is happening there? I mean with her and Bart."

"Sounds like that little discussion they had resulted in some hurt feelings."

"Sounds to me like he put his foot down."

"In true cowboy fashion," Mike said. "You know, thinking about that, whatever happened to the cowboy way, like never hitting a woman?"

"Long gone, Sexy Man. Physical abuse, spousal abuse is always in the news."

"I'd never hit you, no matter what you did."

"If I wrecked your Porsche Carrera 911?"

"Ha, just a piece of metal. Not the cowboy way."

"If I wiped out our checking account?"

"Only money. Not the cowboy way."

Beth was enjoying the little game. "If I insulted you in public, stepped on your ego?"

"We'd talk about it in private. Cowboy way."

Beth thought of the worst: "If I ran away with another man?"

"I'd track you down, strip the guy naked, smear him with honey, and tie him over an anthill. I'd carry you home over the back of my horse, Thunder, and convince you once we were home that I was the best thing that

95

ever happened to you. Cowboy way." A big smile appeared on his face. He then asked, "What if I ran away with another woman?"

Beth responded instantly, "Sexy Man, I'd track you down and shoot you both. Urban cowgirl way."

The statement made them both laugh, and finally Mike said, "Violent femme, huh?"

"I was just joking, Sexy Man, you know that. But really, don't you think it's ironic that in the Old West, the way was to honor women and never harm them, and in today's culture, it's very different?"

"Our culture is very different, for men and women. Life isn't valued as much, I think. Drive-by shootings. Killing someone over a pair of name-brand sneakers. Violence in the schools."

"In the office place, also!"

"So sad." Mike was quiet for a moment, but then said, "That's one of the reasons why I'm happy to be on this vacation with you, the person who means the most to me in this world."

Beth put her hand on his arm. "I feel the same way about you. I'm very happy to share my good times with you."

"And this is a good time. At first I had my doubts," Mike commented, "but thinking about our morning, how magical it was. We didn't see a soul out there on our ride, unless you count the rabbits and gophers."

"And that eagle. Wasn't that marvelous?"

"Exactly. We saw no other human. Think back to Milford. It seems harder and harder to get away from it all, whether you live in a big place or a little one. It's no wonder that people go off, lose it, resort to dire measures to handle their stress."

Beth moved her head up and down slowly, thinking.

"You're right. Life is full of stress. Even for us. We have a wonderful relationship, and still little things make us tense. We're so lucky to have each other."

"So lucky. Every time I see your smiling face, no matter what kind of day I've had, that beautiful smile of yours makes all the bad go away."

"I know how you feel. When I go out into the real world, I see people do the meanest things. Like human life has no value. Then I come home, and there's you. Having you in my life does make all the difference." Beth leaned forward and kissed him. "And that you are so sexy, that makes it all the better." She kissed him again.

"There are a couple of beds right over there," Mike hinted.

"And so forthright with your feelings," Beth added. "After the last few nights, I'd have thought you'd have had your fill of me."

"Oh, Pretty Girl, having my fill of you would be like a bee having too much honey, like a millionaire having too much money." He pulled her to his chest and kissed her. The smell of Euphoria filled his nose. He nuzzled her cheek, and strands of her auburn hair brushed across his face. He put his arms around her shoulders and slid them down to just above her hips. Leaning back, he gazed into her blue/green eyes and whispered, "Having too much of you would be like saying there's too much water in the sea. I can never have too much of you."

She now kissed him. Her mouth open, she ran her tongue around his lips, over his teeth, then with its tip, she met his tongue and circled its tip with hers. Their mouths made a circle that moved in starts and quivers, and through it they exchanged breath in a simple sharing that symbolized a trust only two people in love can share.

"Ah," Mike said, when they separated. "How about

those beds?"

"How about that swim you talked about?" she countered.

He looked at her in disbelief. "Pretty Girl, you feeling OK?"

"I'm hot and dusty."

"But don't you think that water will be cold? Very cold?"

"After that kiss, I'm hot, very hot." She reached up and grabbed the black suit. "And I know you can keep me warm, but you better hurry or I might change my mind. Cowgirl's prerogative." She went to a chair by the wooden table in the center of the floor, sat down, and pulled off her boots. "Hey, Cowpoke, could you help a cowgirl get out of her chaps? In the cowboy way?"

With enthusiasm, he did.

CHAPTER TEN

There was not even a ripple on the lake. It looked like it could be a sheet of glass, and when Beth lowered her leg down off the dock and dipped her toe into the water, she understood why. "Burrr," she said immediately withdrawing her foot. "It's cold."

"I'll keep you warm," Mike reminded her.

"I don't know." She took a step back and wrapped the towel tighter around her.

"It can't be that cold," Mike countered. "Besides, it hot out here. Look, I'm sweating right now. The water'll feel good." He pulled the towel from her.

"You go first," she urged. "I'll come in after you."

"Ho, ho, ho," he replied. "You recall I suggested we stay in the cabin. Try out the bunk beds, remember? What I was thinking would have been something to put in the ole mental scrapbook, but nooooooo, you wanted to go swimming. Your idea, but I thought, 'Hey, that would be even better.' You know how I've been reacting in water lately. This was your idea, so let's go." He dropped his towel, exposing the trunks he wore which were so close to his skin color that it looked like he was nude.

Quickly the memories crossed her mind: the shower, the hot tub. The temperature was in the 80s, but the water said cold, cold, cold. "I don't know." She shivered to il- lustrate her feeling.

Mike suspected the water was cold. It was, after all, a mountain lake, probably fed by ice still melting some- where several thousand feet higher than their current el- evation. But the moment was now, and he was ready. Grabbing Beth around her shoulders, he clutched her to his side, picking her off her feet in the process. Then, taking one giant step, he leapt off the end of the dock.

"Noooooooo," Beth screamed on the way down, but her shout was quickly replaced with "ooooogh," a sound that was swallowed by the chilling water only to become bubbles. As soon as she broke free from his grasp, she kicked herself upward and began yelling as soon as her head broke the surface. "You! You! Wait till I get you!" She slapped at the water and twisted to see where he would emerge.

When Mike surfaced, he was behind her. "Hey, Cowgirl," he called. When she turned around, he splashed water in her face and ducked back under the water. He opened his eyes to see that the lake was crystal clear. He could see Beth's legs in from of him. Immediately, he went forward and grabbed them. Their warmth felt wonderful. He pushed his face against her thigh, where his salt and pepper hair was greeted with one of her hands.

She grabbed him and drew him upward.

He had little choice but to comply.

"Oh, you!" she yelled at him.

He started to laugh.

"You are so funny." She shoved his head underwater. "So funny."

With a lungful of air and freedom to roam, Mike returned to his prior place. Wrapping his arms around her thighs, he nuzzled his face against her skin and blew out a bubble of air. Looking up, he could see it rush its way upward, brushing against her crotch, then stomach and break up as it hit her breasts.

He also saw her hands coming down again and tried to move, but her legs closed quickly, trapping him in her feminine warmth. It was a nest he would have welcomed except his supply of air was running out. He knew she was just playing around, and he knew he could free himself by merely employing his strength, but instead, he inched his chin forward and gently bit at the material of her suit.

She instantaneously released him.

This time when he reached the surface, he was lucky to get a breath of air, because Beth immediately set both her hands on his head and dunked him again. Opening his eyes this time, all he could see were thousands of tiny bubbles, caused as he was suddenly to figure out, by Beth's skilled effort to dive under him. That realization came when he felt her fingers reach inside his suit and yank it down, down past his knees, past his ankles and off his body. Through the clear blue water, he could see her racing away from him like a mermaid, waving his suit at him in the process.

Mike tried to pursue Beth, but he was short on air, so he had to surface. About ten yards away, he saw her, treading water next to the dock and holding his trunks above her head. "Cute, real cute," he said, "why don't you throw those back over here?"

"Why should I?"

"So I don't flash the world? Is that a good answer?"

"Not really. There's no one here except you and me."

Mike said, "Then you take off yours."

"I don't think so."

"Come on. Do it."

"Nah."

"Why?"

"Well, it's not very ladylike, now is it, to strip down to the buff?"

"A cowgirl would do it." Mike egged her on.

"You think? And wouldn't that make the cowboys think she was easy?"

"Only if they saw her."

She waved his suit over her head. "You-hoo, oh Mister Cowboy."

He started to move toward her, saying, "You know it doesn't matter. It's not like they were keeping me warm or anything." He picked up his stroke, swimming her way, keeping his head above water. "In fact, it feels kind of neat. Gives me an idea."

He began to swim faster.

After their seven years together, she had more than an inkling of what his idea was. She turned and swam for the ladder that led up to the dock. Five feet, four, three, two. She reached out her hand and felt the material of her suit begin to move down her body.

With his left hand, Mike reached up and swept the straps off her shoulders. With his right hand, he grabbed at the back of her suit. In a quick tug, he pulled her swimwear down over her thighs and past her knees.

Beth had a hand on the ladder and began to pull herself up, but the further up she went, the further down her suit came. By the time she was up one step, her fanny was shining in the sun. She let go and her body slid back into the chilly water.

Fortunately, Mike was there to catch her, which he eagerly did. "Little scheme backfire on you?" he asked.

She spun around and put her legs around his waist. "Depends on which scheme you're referring to." She squeezed her legs and put her arms around his neck. "Now you just look at the predicament you've gone and gotten us into."

"Me?" he began, but thought better of mounting any argument. "Me, that's what I had planned all along."

"I thought so," Beth cooed, no longer cold, but, to her surprise, feeling the heat starting to grow inside her, like a burning ember. She kissed him. "You are turning into quite the Romeo, a water-soaked one, but Romeo, nonetheless. I'm liking this vacation a lot."

"Only trying to please you, ma'am." Mike tipped a make-believe Stetson.

She splashed water on him and said vivaciously, "I thought I told you not to call me that."

"And what should I call you, ma'am?" He kept up the facade.

She ran her hands over his sides and around to his back. "How about Pretty Girl, the Water Nymph?"

"Water Nymph? How about Beth, My Little Mermaid?"

"Oh, kiss me, fool, and call me what you want. Can't you see I've surrendered?"

"Yeah? Well, where's my trunks?"

"Uh-oh," Beth suppressed a giggle. "I forgot about those. I think I dropped them."

"Funny girl."

"I did, Mike, but wait." She quickly reached down and felt around below his waist. "You mean to tell me you are naked! Nude in front of Pretty Girl, Queen of the Water Nymphs!" She moved her hand around and shrieked. "Oh my, yes, you are naked. Uncovered. Exposed for all my underwater friends to see."

"And what do they see?"

She nuzzled his neck with her chin and said, "Something nice." She felt him. "Very nice." She gently squeezed with her fingers.

With his hand, he did the same to her, asking, "Is it OK for your underwater friends to see you with no clothes on?"

"Of course. They are my subjects."

"Well, I'd like to be your predicate."

"Ha, ha."

"Yes, predicate, a verb, your action verb, the verb that turns you on, starts the action."

She moved her hand around and again squeezed him with her hand. "But with this, I'm not sure how much action where will be."

Now it was his turn to laugh. "Hey, this water is cold!"

"I can tell. What shall we call this? Little worm?"

"Well, as I recall, just last night, it was a Night Crawler."

"The day's young. You never know what could happen," she said with a sly smile. "Let's move over closer to the dock where we might be able to get a handle on this." She pushed off and floated on her back. Her breasts moved along the surface like two silk flowers, her stomach was a pillow of promise.

In a trance, Mike followed in her wake.

The water was no longer cold. Beth's sensual swim had stirred in him a fire that surpassed mortal temperature. His blood was fueled with a lust she had created. What cold there had been was displaced with passion. He was again a night crawler.

When he caught up with her, she grasped his transformation and said, "Ooooh."

There was a need in Mike that he could not control. They were where he could plant his feet on the bottom. He pulled Beth close to him and raised her body up so she rested above his thighs. With an urgency that even surprised him, he drew her down.

When they made contact, his eyes closed and rolled back in his head, and at that exact moment, she shouted, "Wait, did you hear that?" Her body tensed and remained still.

Mike, of course, had heard nothing. At the moment she had called out, a meteor could have landed in the lake and he would have heard nothing. "No, what was it?"

"I don't know. It was over there." She pointed toward an area by the cabin.

"What was it? What'd it sound like?"

"Leaves rustling. Branches moving."

"Can you see anything?"

"No," she answered, "but I heard it."

"It was probably nothing." Mike tried to calm her, and in an attempt to rekindle the passion, pulled her back to his still-ready anatomy.

"Mike, I heard something. I'm sure of it." She pushed away. "Give me my suit."

"Your suit? What about mine?"

She shot him an 'I mean it' look.

"OK," he said, handing her the one-piece. "And mine?"

She grabbed the material and rushed to put it on. "Yours is on the ladder on the end of the dock."

Mike moved to retrieve it when Beth uttered in a panic, "There it is again." She pointed. "Over there!"

Mike became serious. He'd heard it, also. "Come over here," he ordered her. "Move back under the dock."

"You heard it, didn't you?"

He tugged at her and nodded his reply in the affirmative.

"You think it's a cougar? Bart said there were cougars around here."

"I don't know what it is. I didn't see anything. I just heard something. It think it sounded like the rustling of the leaves."

She clung to him. "I'm scared."

"Don't be. I don't think cougars like water." He began to move toward the ladder.

"Where are you going?" Beth demanded, but her voice was full of fear.

"To get my shorts. No matter how safe I might feel, I'll feel a whole lot safer if I'm wearing pants." Mike let go of Beth and quickly swam to get his trunks, which he immediately put on.

As he was making his way back to Beth, they both heard a familiar but very unexpected voice calling, "You-hoo. Anybody here?"

CHAPTER ELEVEN

Back on the front porch of the cabin, the three sat and looked out over the lake and mountains. It was a tranquil time of day when the afternoon was making its decision to head toward evening.

There were puffy clouds forming in the distance, but they seemed to be hardly moving. The sun's rays were filtering through the overhanging tree boughs. The wind was almost nonexistent, and quiet filled the porch like an invisible visitor everyone wanted to acknowledge but no one dared to approach.

Beth sat with her arms around her knees, hugging them close to her chest. As she looked out over the scenery, her mind was wavering between embarrassment and pride. She suspected Rainbow had been witness to all that had happened in the lake. *I knew we should have been more careful,* she told herself, Mike *just doesn't think with his head sometimes, at least the one on his shoulders.*

Beth suspected Rainbow had watched it all, and the thought made her angry, but then a uplifting notion flashed through her mind, and she reasoned, *But she got quite an eyeful if she did, and what an eyeful it must have been. Now she'll see that I can be just as wild as she appears to be. No one can take my* Mike *to the sexual height I can take him. No one!* And then a wide grin filled her face.

Mike leaned against the cabin wall, arms crossed over his chest, hat pulled down over his blue eyes. What an afternoon he had had. He felt cold, not from the temperature but from the situation he had just worked through. On the one hand, he felt guilty that he had taken the play in the lake too far. But, thinking of Beth, he said to himself, *she just excites me so much sometimes I just can't stop. Once she gets me going, there's no pulling back.* And then he cast his gaze to the auburn-haired woman who had interrupted his foray into the land of the erotic. *What did she see?* he wondered. *Everything? A little? Nothing? Should I just out and ask her? Wouldn't that clear the air? No, not a good idea. We'll just have to wonder.*

He rearranged his arms and thought of Beth: *I'm sorry she was put in an awkward position. I should apologize to her when we're alone, but even if Rainbow saw everything, so what? We didn't do anything wrong. It's not like we planned it. If Rainbow saw us, it was by accident. I can only hope she got a good idea of just how hot we are for each other.* Beth *can get me going anywhere, even in a lake that's water temperature is slightly above freezing.* A smile formed on his lips.

Rainbow's back was against one of the porch supports. Her face was a picture of contentment; however, her thoughts were not so sublime. *That Bart, that Bart, that Bart!* summed up the conversation running its course in her brain. She'd busted her butt racing over here to find him, to talk to him, to fix what she could and see what he'd do to fix what was left. Then, when she'd gotten here, all she'd found were these two doing their thing in the water.

At another time in her life, it might have been very entertaining to just stay hidden and watch, but today she was really in no mood for it, so she had interrupted. And although she knew that it was fine for Bart to leave guests at the cabin while he went off to check on things, she also knew it was odd that he'd been gone so long. Finally, she broke the silence by saying, "What time did Bart say he'd be back?"

"In a couple of hours," Beth answered, even though they'd already told Rainbow all the details of Bart's departure and his specific instructions for them to stay put.

"And where'd he say he was going?" Rainbow asked.

"Up to the upper pasture, to fix a fence. Wasn't that what he said?" Beth looked to Mike for support.

"Yes, that's what he said, and that he had to check on some cattle," Mike confirmed. "Told us to wait here till he got back."

Rainbow nodded and thought for a moment, then asked, "Did he say anything else? Anything about poachers specifically?"

Beth and Mike were quiet for a second remembering the conversations they'd had during the day. Mike said, "While we were on the ride over to here, we saw an eagle, remember Beth?"

"Do I? It was beautiful."

"And then Bart told us that he's seen poachers shooting at them and that it's a Federal law to kill eagles."

A frown appeared on Rainbow's face. "Did he see a poacher? Did he look around, you know, turn Bullet around so he could see all around him?"

Mike could sense her concern. "No, we kind of slowed down. But all we watched was the bird."

"You watched the bird. You didn't watch Bart, in other words. Man," she said with concern.

"What's wrong?" Beth asked.

"Nothing, probably nothing." Rainbow sighed.

"Sure sound like something," Mike ventured.

"He'll be back soon," Rainbow responded. "Come on, let's go get the horses ready." She stood and motioned for them to follow.

"You sure everything's OK?" Beth questioned as she

rose. "Has he been gone too long? You think something's happened to him?"

"He said there were cougars around here." Mike told her. "Could. . ?"

Rainbow cut him off by saying over her shoulder, "Bart can take care of himself. He'll be back soon."

With worry working its way into their psyches, they got the horses set for the trip back, and by the time they were ready to mount, Mike asked, "Are we going to leave before he gets back?"

The clopping on the trail removed any need for an answer.

"Hey, y'all!" Bart called as he pulled on the reins and stopped Bullet in front of them. "When did you get here?" he spoke to Rainbow.

"Been awhile," she replied. "You OK?"

"Me? Sure. Why?"

"You been gone a while."

"Nothing to worry about. Had a bit of fence to mend, a stray to lasso, a bit of this and that. You know what it's like to be away on the range."

"Away on the range, huh?" Rainbow repeated his statement. "See anything, anyone unusual?"

A strange smile crossed Bart's lips, and then he said, "Nope, didn't see a soul."

Rainbow nodded, but did not speak.

"You ready to head on back?" Bart asked.

"I figured we better get a move on if we're to make the bonfire tonight," Rainbow said as she looked at Beth and Mike. "You two are going to the bonfire, aren't you?"

"If it's on the schedule, we're planning on doing it," Mike responded.

"That's good," said Rainbow, "because Bitty and Wally put on a great bonfire. The best around. You don't want to miss it."

"You're right. We don't," acknowledged Beth. She wondered if the words came out as she intended, to suggest everything was fine. There was still tension in the air, and now added to that was her own worry. Just what was out here on the range?

This wild west stuff was starting to feel a little too real.

Whitey was waiting for them when they brought the horses back to the stables. As the riders dismounted, Bart said, "Well, that was a great day. You two are fun to ride with."

"And fun to watch," Rainbow threw in with a sly smile that made Mike and Beth wonder about her intent. "But the fun's just beginning. For now, as promised, Whitey's going to show you how to groom your horses."

"You're not going to show them how to do that?" Bart asked.

Rainbow answered, "No, Whitey can take care of it, can't you, Whitey?"

"No problem, or how they say it south of the border, da nada," the ranch hand replied.

"Si, Senor," Bart said, "I know you can. But usually Rainbow does it."

"Well, today," Rainbow spoke slowly, "Rainbow has something else she wants to do. And it involves you. Now let Whitey teach them the grooming. You and I have some talking to do. Come on." She handed her reins to Whitey, turned on her heels and brushed past Bart, grabbing his hand in the process and yanking him into motion.

"See y'all at the bonfire," she called to Mike and Beth.

"Yeah," was their mutual reply.

For the second time, Rainbow and Bart had exited suddenly, needing to talk.

Whitey didn't speak, but motioned with his head for Beth and Mike to follow him with their horses to the grooming area. Once there, he whispered, "When she gets like that, best to give her a wide path. She got quite a streak in her. Not that Bart don't, too. He can be a mean one."

Whitey helped them take off the saddles and directed them toward the grooming tools, showing them where to stand and what to use by demonstrating on Bullet and Lightning. He worked on two horses while they mimicked his motions on their own mounts.

"Rainbow seemed a bit upset at the cabin," Mike said.

"Yep, she tore outta here lookin' for y'all," Whitey told them. "I told her where I thought ya might be, only not like Bart tole me to tell her." He chuckled. "I sure don't want to get on the wrong side of her, if ya know what I mean."

"We get the picture," Beth answered.

"Like I said," Mike said, "She seemed upset. Especially after she asked about poachers. Bart mentioned them because we saw an eagle."

"Bart don't take kindly to poachers." Whitey talked as he ran the curry over the side of Bullet's withers. "That's a fact. She tell you what happened, did she?"

"No, not really," Mike responded, "She got this look on her face, that's all."

"Well, I don't know it's my place to be telling tales,

but Bart killed a man a while back. You heard about that?"

The look on the guests' faces was his answer.

Whitey couldn't resist telling the story, so he went on, "Oh, yeah, several years back, there were some guys shooting eagles, selling their feathers on the black market or something like that. I understand some folks'll pay mucho dinero for the tail feathers of an eagle. The sheriff and game warden kept finding dead eagles up on the trail. Well, the way I hear it happened, Bart was up past Cougar Point one afternoon and heard some shooting up in the trees. Coulda been some hunters after deer, but he looked up and saw a bald eagle soaring then heard more shots. When the eagle dipped and swooped off, he knew what was happening."

Whitey quit talking and walked over to Mike, took the brush from his hand and said, "Here, go like this." Whitey ran the brush in long strokes across Thunder's back. "Go easy. He'll like it better." He looked at Beth and praised her. "See, she's got it."

He went back to Bullet and continued his tale, "So Bart high-tailed it up the mountain and come across these two wahoos. They were sitting on a rock still shootin' when he comes up on them, and Bart yells at 'em and one of the guys takes aim at Bart. In a flash, Bart slides his rifle up and draws a bead on the gringo." Whitey positioned his arms as if they were holding a rifle. "Bart's got the guy covered, and he yells at them, 'Put down you guns!' But instead, the gringo shoots at Bart. Bart said he heard the bullet whiz by his ear." Whitey ducked for effect, but then stood up and resumed the position of holding his imaginary rifle. "Blam!" he shouted, "Bart shot the fool. Dead in the chest. The other poacher jumped from the rock, and Bart took off after him. The guy turned to fire, and Bart shot at him too, but the guy tripped on a root and fell backwards, tumbled down a slope and went over a cliff. The sheriff's search party found him the next day with a broken neck."

"Wow," Mike uttered. "The first guy was dead?"

"Yep. Both of 'em. Really, Bart just killed the one. The other I figure was a accident."

"Did Bart get charged? Was there a trial?" Beth asked.

"Self-defense. The poacher shot at him. There was actually a nick in Bart's hat where the bullet went. An inch closer, and he'd a been a dead man hisself." Whitey took off his hat to show them how close the bullet had come. "And the sheriff found a bag of eagle feathers at the guy's camp. Two stupid, sorry losers if you ask me."

"And Bart took it fine?" asked Beth.

"Bart's one hard dude. One very hard dude."

"Sounds like it," she commented.

"I sure'd never want to make him mad. Understand he's got quite a temper and the muscle to back it up. But then again, there's nobody I'd rather have by my side in a fight."

"I can see that," Mike said, "How long's he been at the Triple Z?"

"He was here when I got here. That was three years ago." He handed Mike a bottle of liniment and a rag. "Here ya go. Wipe 'em down with this to finish. They'll love it."

He gave a rag to Beth then continued talking, "I don't know how long Bart's been around here exactly. He's been around though, that's for sure. Rodeo rider, cowpoke, rancher, bush pilot, hunting guide, and that's all after he dropped out of society."

Mike took a whiff of the liquid and said, "Hey, this doesn't smell half bad."

"The horses sure like it is all I know," Whitey said.

"They say some cowboys wear it for aftershave. Me, I prefer Old Spice."

Mike laughed. "I prefer Kouros myself." He then asked, "You said Bart was a drop out? What'd you mean?"

"Bart's been around is all I can say," Whitey offered. "Something about professional baseball, something about Vietnam, about Wall Street, about a wife and kid, long story so's I hear. One I can't rightly tell."

"I hear what you're saying," Mike said.

"Near's as I can say, he made his way out here and linked up with Mr. Wally and Miss Bitty and then Rainbow came to likin' him and now he's mostly happy. End of story, eh?"

Beth spoke up, "Or just the beginning."

"Anyways, I got to go put some stuff together for the bonfire tonight. Red Deer's comin' I hear. You know him?"

"No," Beth answered.

"American Indian, storyteller, medicine man. Should be quite a night, but now I got to go. You two put yer horses back in their stalls. You can handle that, can't cha?"

"Sure can, Whitey," Mike promised. "You go do what you need to do."

After the ranch hand walked out of the stables, Mike said to Beth, "Wow, Bart killed a man!"

"Not something we ought to talk about."

"That's wild. He's like a real cowboy, isn't he?"

She nodded her head. "If having tragedy in your life makes you a cowboy."

"That's not tragedy. It's excitement, adventure."

"I don't think we know the full story," she cautioned him and then, as if reading his mind said, "Nor is it our business to ask."

They finished with the horses, led them to the stalls, and came back to put away the grooming tools. Mike asked, "So what do you think Bart and Rainbow had to talk about?"

Beth thought a moment before speaking. "They aren't happy with something."

The thought crossed Mike's mind to tell Beth he was sorry about what had happened at the lake. He stepped over to her, put his arms around her and drew her close to his chest. He inhaled deeply and said, "Ummmm, that does smell good."

"You're funny. The liniment? Better than Euphoria?"

He ran his fingers along her smooth neck and leaned his head closer, inhaling again. "Ummmm, I like it." He kissed her skin and asked, "Do you like it?"

"Your kisses or the smell?"

He kissed her again, behind the ear. "Both?"

She twisted her head so her lips were next to his, "Yes, both." Her lips pressed against his in embrace. She held onto him, her mouth to his, until she had no more breath, then released, inhaling fully the smell into her nostrils. "Oh, my, I see what you mean. It makes me dizzy almost. I like it."

"My kisses or the smell?"

Beth pushed him backward with her hips, nudging his body toward a pole by the edge of the stall. She could feel the heat rise from him, feel the strength of him, feel the swell of emotion coming from him. She put her arms onto his biceps and pulled herself into his chest, pressed her breasts against him, brought her stomach and thighs so they rested flat against his. "Oh, you," she cooed, "this is just how you made me feel this afternoon. You get me so hot."

"This afternoon," Mike said, considering mounting his apology, but before he could go any further, Beth wrapped her right leg around his left, curling her calf around behind his knee, pulling his body into hers even further.

"This afternoon at the lake only lacked one thing," she spoke for him, "and we should make amends for that now." With her right hand she reached up over his left shoulder, took a hold of the ladder leading to the hayloft, and pulled herself upward.

Mike looked up and saw the rungs of the ladder leading to the upper loft. Then he looked at Beth.

She offered no words, simple pulled harder which caused her body to rise, knocking Mike's hat off in the process. Immediately, her breasts were pressed to his face, and she put her left hand onto the ladder and hung there, letting her weight rest fully on Mike, letting the softness of her chest lie warmly across his cheeks.

Mike required no encouraging to quickly unbutton the blouse she wore and find her skin with his mouth.

Hanging by both hands, Beth wrapped her legs around Mike's back and ground her loins against his chest. It was a moment of rapture and wave after wave of pleasure rose up her spine.

Mike put his hands on her bottom, giving her some support, squeezing for his own pleasure, but before he knew it, she began to go higher, inching herself upward until her bare stomach was passing before his face. Mike kissed it, put his lips on it and sucked at her belly button, licked the salty moisture from it.

Beth had somehow found a lower rung with her right foot, and she used it for support. Her left leg she raised till it rested on Mike's right shoulder. She was able to move her hips back far enough for him to move his head forward where he placed his lips on the denim material just below her zipper, opened his mouth, and exhaled a breath of warm air.

The hot warmth about made her lose her grip.

Fortunately, Mike had wrapped his arm around her right leg which was all she needed to maintain her stability. Nevertheless, the second shot of air he forced past her jeans and panties made her go limp.

It was all she could do to hold on as her body shuddered. When Beth regained her sense of control, she gently ground her hips against him, but then pulled herself up, scaling the ladder to the upper level. "Come with me," she told him.

Mike eagerly followed. By the time his head popped up past the floor of the hayloft, Beth was already seated in a pile of hay and pulling off her boots. By the time Mike reached her, she was pulling off her blue jeans. By the time he stood over her, she was lying back wearing only her black panties and a wide smile. He stared at the two luscious mounds of her breasts, then looked back into her welcoming blue/green eyes. He felt a heat throbbing within him from the need for her.

Beth ran her fingers through her auburn hair, looked up at Mike and said, "If I'm gonna find that needle in this haystack, you better get to losing it. "

"Pronto," Mike replied as he tore at his clothes to release his needle.

"I've got a special place for you to hide it, Sexy Man" she cooed. "Right over here." She ran her hands down her sides, over her stomach and down inside the thin strip of material that was her panties.

"Oh, I know you do."

Raising her hips, she slid off the flimsy material. She was already covered in a thin film of perspiration from Mike's hot breath on her there. Her loins ached for him. She arched her hips toward him, suggestively.

Peeling off his pants and underwear, Mike gladly

placed himself on top of her, eager for the fit of their two bodies.

Their hearts raced in anticipation.

The hay was soft, the air was warm, the smells of the stable and the liniment and their own two bodies was intoxicating. A gentle rocking lead to steady heaving. The boards of the loft went to creaking. The motion sent dust and bits of straw down between the cracks in the flooring. The particles spun and swirled through beams of light toward the ground while Mike and Beth raced toward the fulfillment only love can bring. With a crashing of emotions, they shivered in ecstasy and clung to each other in the quiet afterglow.

Wrenching them from their bliss, however, was a highly unexpected and all-too-familiar voice calling, "You-hoo, anybody there?"

"Uh, yeah," Mike yelled down as he and Beth grabbed for their clothes, "it's us."

"Mike? Beth?" the female voice replied. "Are you up in the hayloft?"

They heard the ladder squeak, saw it shake from the weight of Rainbow climbing it. Frantically they pulled on their clothes.

Mike was quickly tugging on his pants, grasping for his shirt.

Beth furiously worked her buttons on her blouse then glanced down at her side to see her panties in the hay pile. She snatched them up and stuck them in her jeans' pocket just as she saw Rainbow's head appear at the opening of loft. She cast a glance at Mike and was happy to see he was fully dressed, too.

"I was getting some stuff for the bonfire tonight, and I thought I heard someone up here. It's you two, huh? Well, I'll be."

You'll be a colossal pain in the butt, Mike *thought to himself,* but said to Rainbow, "Yes, just us."

How could this have happened twice to us? Beth was thinking, but instead said to Rainbow, "We were just looking for a needle up here."

"I hope you found it," Rainbow said.

"I think we did," Mike replied. There was a gleam in his blue eyes.

CHAPTER TWELVE

The two of them once again found themselves nestled in a bed of hay, only this time it was drawn by a team of horses. Bitty and Wally were on the seat up front. Bart and Rainbow were following on Bullet and Beauty. Everyone was on their way to the bonfire, a weekly ritual at the Triple Z. Only this week was extra special because this week Red Deer would be there telling tales of American Indian lore.

"No ghost stories," was how Bitty had put it. "Some folks love to tell ghost stories around the fire. But Red Deer is uncommon. He has a scary tale or two, but he don't do them much. He'll be fun. He's authentic."

The wagon moved along over the rutted road, jostling its passengers which threw them closer together. Mike and Beth lay back on a plaid blanket.

"Hey," Wally yelled after going over a pothole that bounced everyone on the wagon, "that'll get you to hold onto each other."

"They don't have a problem doing that," chimed in Rainbow.

Beth shot Rainbow a catlike grin and drew Mike closer with her arm.

"Oh yeah, I like that," Mike said into Beth's ear. His arm was around her back, and he squeezed her arm with his fingers.

The sun was on its way to setting. A blaze of red spread out over the horizon. The temperature was cooling just a bit, making it perfect to cuddle. A gentle breeze was picking up.

"Time of the day for the devil to come out," Bitty

said. "Least that's what the locals say about this time of day. When the sun's going and the night's coming on. A transition between living and dead, is how they put it."

Wally gave her a look like she was crazy. "You come up with the darndest things."

She gave him a serious look in reply. "I don't make 'em up. People tell 'em to me. Doesn't it make sense? If you were a ghost, when would you make your move? Right when darkness comes makes the most sense to me."

"OK, OK, I see your point," Wally said. "But let's let Red Deer do the storytelling this week. OK?" He reached under the front seat and immediately music began to play Friends in Low Places by Garth Brooks.

"Just like being in your Porsche Carrera 911," Beth whispered to Mike.

The sound was coming from each end of the wagon, and Mike could just make out the screened face of a speaker in the corner. "Pretty nice," he shouted to Wally.

"It's no quadraphonic masterpiece, but folks seem to like it," the owner responded. "It's all on cassette tape. Hope you like it."

"And if you don't," Bitty added, "We'll be at the bonfire soon."

"I'm sure we'll love it," Beth replied.

"Sing along if you like." Wally told them.

All of Me by Willie Nelson started up, and Mike could not contain himself. He began to sing, "All of me, why not take all of me?" and continued to follow the words, all the while taking Beth's hand and pulling it down below the blanket that covered them from the waist down.

She followed along with the words and gave him a quick thrill as she let him place her hand over his inner thigh. Rubbing ever so slightly, she leaned her mouth to his ear and said quietly, "I thought I took all of you this afternoon?"

"Yes, yes that's right, and all of me is for you, anytime you want it take it," he told her.

Beth glanced off to the right and saw Rainbow looking directly at her. The smile on Rainbow's face made Beth wonder if she had spoken too loudly.

Rainbow clicked at Beauty and the two of them moved forward.

What of it, Beth said to herself, *at least I'm not fighting with my man.* She moved even closer to Mike, letting her hand rest fully on him, feeling the heat rise off this man who made her so happy.

The wagon rounded a bend in the road. Over the speakers came the words to Home on the Range, and everyone began to sing: "Oh, give me a home, where the buffalo roam, and the deer and the antelope play. Where seldom is heard, a discouraging word, and the sky's are not cloudy all day. Home, home on the range. Where the deer and the antelope play. Where seldom is heard, a discouraging word, and the sky's are not cloudy all day." They sang till the end.

"Yes, sir, what a song," Wally called back from his seat as he reduced the volume on the next tune. "Everybody loves to sing it, but I bet you don't know it was written by a fella who ran away from his wife!"

"Wally!" Bitty shouted. "Now you quit it right now. Nobody wants to hear that story."

"Oh, sure they do. It's a good story," Wally went on. "This fella from out East, he ran away from his wife and wrote that song, Home on the Range. Fella's name was Higley, Brewster Higley, I believe. His wife was a real nag, was the version I heard, so he left her. Wrote the song. Just listen to it. The words make sense. Listen," he began to sing, 'where seldom is heard, a discouraging word.' That's about her nagging at him."

Bitty slapped Wally on the shoulder. "Wally! You know I hate that story."

"But, Bitty," Wally said through a chuckle, "I ain't makin' it up."

"Maybe not," she said sternly, "but that doesn't mean you have to tell it. You know I hate that story. It's such a nice song and you go and ruin it."

By this time everyone was laughing but Bitty. "That's OK, Bitty," Mike called up to her. "It's still a pretty song."

Bitty looked back at him, "But he doesn't have to tell it." She slapped Wally again, saying, "You old coot!"

"And you're an old loon," Wally said, "But we're in love, and that's what counts."

"Awww," Beth let out. "You two are sweet."

Wally put his arm around Bitty and said, "Sweet as honey."

"Yeah," Bitty agreed, "We got it good."

"And that said," said Wally, "it's time to start the show. Whoa!" he yelled at the team. "Pull up!"

The wagon had come to a grove of sycamore trees alongside the stream. Colored-paper lanterns aglow with candles hung from wires stretched between tree trunks. Picnic tables were spaced about. People were talking and eating. A small corral was filled with horses. Bitty said, "Good, I see that Red Deer is here."

"Won't be but a short time before we start then," Wally commented. "Y'all jump down, and we'll go on over and find a spot around the bonfire."

Beth looked around. She was puzzled. "What bonfire?"

"Oh, some people call it a bonfire, some a campfire." Wally patted Beth on the shoulder. "You come on over, and we'll grab a bite to eat and get something to drink."

The lanterns made the whole area festive, Beth had to admit, but she could see no fire. She and Mike followed Wally and Bitty to a table where barbecue, vegetables, and beverages were served. Whitey and other ranch hands were about. So were their dates or mates and families. Wally and Bitty insisted that the bonfire night was not just for guests but for the entire ranch family, and each week the grove was full. The food was good, the beer was cold, and the talk was lively and nonstop. Then as the light of day quickly slipped away, a tall man dressed in traditional American Indian attire walked toward them.

"Red Deer," Wally said, "These are my guests this week. Beth Butts and Mike Butts."

"Beth," Beth said as she extended her hand, "Call me Beth."

Mike then shook Red Deer's hand and said, "Mike. Good to meet you."

"Likewise," said the storyteller, "Welcome to the land my people call home. I'm glad you're here." He looked at Wally and said, "It's time to begin."

Wally nodded and waved his hands to signal everyone to gather.

"Follow me," Red Deer said to Beth and Mike. He strode toward the center of the site, and they followed. Red Deer motioned for them to stop, and then Beth could see the stack of wood in front of them. Briskly, all the other people came up, and soon there was a circle of people around the wood. "Sit, everyone be seated," Red Deer directed.

Red Deer remained standing. On the ground to his right were Wally and Bitty. To his left were Beth and Mike, with Rainbow and Bart next on the ring around the stack of wood.

Raising his hands to the sky, Red Deer called in a loud, baritone voice, "Welcome, all, to these most sacred of lands, where we gather in friendship, where we come in joy, where we shall learn of old and make of new. Welcome."

Still standing, Red Deer lowered his hands, put them to his sides, and made fists. For a few moments he was quiet, then he started to utter sounds that might have been a chant, might have been a song, might have been a mantra. In the early stages of darkness, his voice called into the night. Whatever the sound was, it drew the attention of all, all that is except Rainbow who had heard it before and had something else on her mind. With stealth, she slid her right hand along the ground until it found Mike's leg. Then with little subtlety, she ran her fingers along the underside of his thigh.

With his left hand, Mike reached down to see what was happening, and when his hand found Rainbow's, he was shocked. As inconspicuously as he could, he pushed it away, but it came back, this time going even further up his thigh.

Red Deer's singing became louder. All eyes and ears were focused on him, except two people's. In a hushed tone, Mike said to Rainbow, "What are you doing?"

"Giving you some encouragement," she whispered so only he could hear. "You're insatiable. I saw you."

He held her hand in his. Pointedly, he said, "Stop it."

"In the lake, in the loft, how about with me?"

"Stop."

She squirmed her hand free and squeezed his leg.

He slapped her fingers. The sound could be heard by others.

"What was that?" Beth asked.

Mike answered, "A mosquito."

"Did you get it?"

Rainbow did not withdraw her hand but instead pinched Mike.

He slapped her hand harder and said, "I think I did that time."

Whether the little exchange disturbed Red Deer was not clear, but at that moment, he ended his chanting and sank into a cross-legged position on the ground. He said, "It is time to tell the story of fire."

Rainbow leaned close to Mike and softly hissed.

Mike chose not to respond.

Red Deer's voice bellowed, "The stories of my people are the stories of all people. They are the stories of my father, of my grandfather and his father's fathers. They are the stories of all time and for all time, and I come now to tell you how it was that fire came to the people of the land.

"In the beginning of the world, there was no fire. People were cold. At night, they could not see. And if they found something that didn't eat them first, they ate it raw because they had no fire to cook it. It was a cold, sad time.

"And this was true of all People: the Bird People, the Animal People, and the Human People. Only the Gods, who lived in the world beyond the sky, had fire, and one day while fighting they let fly a lightning bolt with went to earth and struck a sycamore tree on an island in the middle of the water. Fire started in the bottom of that sycamore tree, a tree much like those around us tonight."

As if on cue, a breeze caused the leaves of the trees to rustle.

"All the People knew that the fire was there. They could see smoke rising from the top of the tree. But they could not get to it. They could not cross the water. So they held a council to decide what to do.

"The Animal and Bird People took the lead. The Human People did not speak. They stood back. 'Life is not good,' the Animal and Bird People decided, 'if it is cold and miserable.' They decided that they must have fire.

"But how could they get it? Who would get it? All who could fly or swim came forth. Much talk was made. Who should have the honor?

"A small voice came from the large crowd. It was Grandmother Spider who said, 'I can do it! Let me try!' But then Opossum began to speak. 'I, Opossum, am a great chief of the animals. I am a great hunter. I will swim to the island, and I will take the fire and carry it back in the bushy hair on my tail.' It was well known that Opossum had the furriest tail of all the animals, so he was selected.

"Opossum went to the island and found the fire. He picked up a small piece of burning wood, and stuck it in the hair of his tail, which immediately began to smoke, then flame. Opossum ran for the water and jumped in, but every bit of hair had burned from his tail, and to this day, opossums have no hair on their tails at all.

"Another council was called and again many volunteered. Grandmother Spider again said, 'Let me go! I can do it.' But instead, the Crow said, 'I am large and strong. I can fly and get the fire.' He was selected.

"At that time Crow was pure white, and he had the most beautiful singing voice of all the birds. He flew across the water and reached the top of the sycamore tree. It was a long flight, so he sat there on the top branch wondering what to do. While he sat there thinking, the heat from the fire scorched all his feathers black. And he breathed so much smoke that when he tried to sing, all that came out was a harsh, 'Caw! Caw!' The poor Crow flew back home without the fire.

"A great trouble settled over the council. They talked and talked. They considered what to do. The decided to try again, and again the Grandma Spider volunteered, saying, 'Let me go get the fire. I can do it.' But Buzzard stepped up. Buzzard was very proud and very pretty. He said, 'I am bigger than Crow. I can fly faster and farther. I will fly to the island and put the fire in the beautiful, long feathers on my head.' It is a shame to say, but none of the People yet understood the nature of fire.

"So Buzzard flew to the island on his powerful wings, swooped down and picked up a small piece of burning ember, and hid it in his head feathers. Off he went, but Buzzard's head began to smoke and flames burned away his feathers! Buzzard was left with a bald head that was red and blistered. To this day, buzzards have naked heads that are bright red and blistered.

"One more council was called. This time the leaders said, "Opossum has failed. Crow and Buzzard have failed. Who shall we send to get the fire?

"Scurrying forward on all eight of her legs, tiny Grandmother Spider shouted with all her might, 'I can do it! Let me try, please.' The leaders had a big talk, and although they thought the little spider had little chance of success, it was agreed that she should have her turn.

"Grandmother Spider looked then like she does to-day. She had a small body held up by two sets of four skinny legs. The first thing she did was walk on those legs to a stream where she found clay. With her front legs, she made a tiny clay container and a lid that fit on it per-fectly. In the lid was a little notch for air. She put the container on her back, climbed the highest tree there was, and then began spinning a web. Faster and faster her legs worked till she had enough silk spun to cast it out into the wind. A strong gust caught it and whisked it to the island where it caught onto the sycamore tree. To the amazement of everyone watching, she then tiptoed on her spun thread of silk until she came to the island.

"Once there, she took a tiny piece of fire, put it in the container, and covered it with the lid. Then she walked back on tiptoe along the web until she came to the People. Since they couldn't see any fire, they said with great disappointment, 'Oh, no, Grandmother Spider has failed.'

"Oh no,' she informed them. 'I have the fire!' She lifted the pot from her back, and then took the lid from the pot. Instantly, the fire flamed up, and all the People went, 'Awwww.'

"Everyone rushed forth to congratulate Grandmother Spider. Everyone wanted to feel the wonderful warmth of the fire. Then another council was called, and the Bird and Animal People began to decide who would get to be the keeper of fire. Bear said, 'I am big and strong. I'll take it!' but when he put his paws on the fire, he burned them and proclaimed, 'Fire is was not for animals, for look what happened to Opossum, look what happened to my paws!'

"The Screech Owl said, 'I should keep it because I am wise,' but when he took a closer look at it he burned his eyes so bad that they turned red like they are today. He said, 'Fire is not for the birds. Look what has happened to Crow and Buzzard and me.'

"Then a small voice from the back said, 'We will take it, if Grandmother Spider will help.' The timid humans, whom none of the animals or birds thought much of, were volunteering to tend the fire.

"Since the Bird People and the Animal People did not want to keep the fire, they agreed to let the Human

People have it.

"So Grandmother Spider taught the Human People how to feed the fire sticks and put wood on it to keep it from dying. She showed them how to keep the fire safe in a circle of stone so it couldn't escape and hurt them or their homes. And while she was at it, she taught the humans about pottery made of clay and fire, and about weaving and spinning, at which Grandmother Spider was an expert.

"And today, My People remember Grandmother Spider. We make a design to decorate our homes. It's a picture of Grandmother Spider with her two sets of legs up, two down, and there's a fire symbol on her back. We do not ever want our children to ever forget to honor Grandmother Spider, Firebringer!

"And that is how we got fire."

As the final word left his mouth, a hush rose from those in the circle because with his last word, an orange flame rose from the center of the stack of wood and quickly spread upward. Most had seen it before and knew the ignition was the result of simple electricity: a switch was thrown which caused a spark the made a wad of cloth soaked in mineral spirits to burst into flame. But even for those who knew it was coming, the sight of fire bursting forth was wondrous.

Beth and Mike sat there with their mouths open in surprise.

Applause came from everyone around the fire.

"And thus are the words of My People," Red Deer said in acknowledgment.

"Tell us another," Wally called out.

"Yeah," added a ranch hand.

"I have so many," Red Deer said. "Which one should I tell?"

Bart spoke up. "Tell us about the cougar. Our two guests were up at Cougar Point. I think they'd like to hear about the cougar."

"Yes, that would be good, then, Bart," Red Deer replied. "And I will tell about the cougar if," he paused for effect, "if you tell the next story."

"Me?" Bart answered, "Why I don't have anything to tell."

"You know you do," Red Deer told him. "I want to hear about your great-granddad. You tell that one."

"And you'll tell about the cougar?"

"It's a deal."

"That's good for us," Bitty said, "but while you are telling that story, me and Rainbow are gonna go get some fixin's for some s'mores. OK?" She stood up. "You go on with the storytelling. We'll listen while we get the treats ready."

Rainbow rose up onto one knee and twisted toward Mike, whispering, "Care to come and help me?" She could see him roll his eyes at her, so she leaned the other way and kissed Bart on the cheek, saying, "I'll be listening. So, don't leave anything out, 'cause you know how excited I get when I hear about Black Bart."

"Right," he replied sarcastically.

"So you went to Cougar Point?" Red Deer asked Beth.

She nodded.

"We used to have many cougar around these parts. They used to range all across all of the country. They like the mountains here. A cougar is not a big cat by some standards. The average male weighs around 150 pounds. Can stretch up to seven feet long. His head is kind of small for his body, but his feet are large, good for climbing, walking on rocks and snow, and tearing into flesh.

His claws are long and sharp. What else? His tail is more that half the length of his body. It's long and pretty.

"They are also called pumas and mountain lions and wildcats. They live mostly on deer, but ranchers will tell you that cougars don't mind a meal of beef now and then. Horses are also at risk, especially colts. Cougars are mostly nocturnal, but the bigger ones, the ones that settle in and get territorial, will come out in the daytime. Will they attack a man? Let's face it, they'll attack anything if they're cornered, protecting their territory, or hungry.

"As to the story Bart has asked for, he seems to like it. There must be a reason for that. I will tell it." Red Deer raised his hands up to the sky and chanted for a moment, then began, "The stories of my people are the stories of all people. They are the stories of my father, of my grandfather and his father's fathers. They are the stories of all time and for all time, and I come now to tell you the story of the cougar and the bear.

"One day Cougar and his son were out hunting, looking for something to take home to Cougar's wife. While they were gone, Bear came to Cougar's camp and saw Cougar's wife there. The Bear immediately fell in love with her. 'I wish I could have her for my wife,' he thought. Then he walked over to where she was sitting. In only a short time, he proposed that she run away with him. She saw how big and pretty the Bear was. She thought to herself, 'He can provide much food for me.' She made up her mind and consented to run away with the Bear.

"When Cougar and his son returned from hunting, Cougar could not find his wife. He looked throughout the camp, but she was not there. He thought to himself, 'I wonder if she could have run away with that Bear?' He and his son looked around some more. At first Cougar and his son could find no tracks, but eventually they picked up the couple's trail.

"Very angry by now, Cougar followed the tracks deep into the forest, out into the plains. As night fell, a high wind began to blow which wiped out most of the tracks. Cougar and his son slept, but Cougar dreamed only of finding his wife and the Bear.

"The next morning, Cougar and his son picked up the trail again and followed the tracks. 'Perhaps they are sleeping in those rocks up there," he thought. He moved closer, and he heard voices and recognized them as his wife's and the Bear's.

"Cougar sent his son to circle back behind the rocks, approaching from the other side of the woods to force the Bear out toward Cougar who approached from the plains.

"Cougar's wife suspected Cougar would try to find them. She said to the Bear, 'Cougar is very strong.'

"The Bear boasted, 'That may be, but I am stronger.' To show her, he grabbed a cedar tree and pulled it from the ground.

"She shook her heard. 'Cougar is stronger than that,' said the wife.

"All of a sudden, Cougar's son attacked, catching the Bear off guard. The Bear had his moccasins off when the son attacked. Quickly he put on his moccasins, but in his haste he put them on the wrong feet. Then, not knowing who was coming up behind him, he ran forward, right into Cougar who was coming from the front.

"The two wrestled, and Cougar threw the Bear to the ground. The Bear rose up again and charged at Cougar, but Cougar was ready. With one of his huge paws, Cougar lashed at the side of the Bear's face, and when the Bear stopped to see if he was bleeding, which he was, Cougar sank his fangs into the back of the Bear's neck. The Bear stood up on his hind legs, but the moccasins were on the wrong feel which confused the Bear. With his mighty hind legs, Cougar pushed the Bear forward. Bear tumbled down against a rock and broke his back.

"Cougar's wife came running over. She was saying, 'I knew you were stronger.' But Cougar sent her away into the woods, letting her know that he did not want her for his wife anymore. Cougar and his son then left on another hunting trip to find a new wife and home for themselves.

"And thus are the words of My People," Red Deer said to finish.

Applause again went around the circle.

"A simple tale like so many," Red Deer offered. He looked at Bart and said, "Now is your turn."

"And those rocks in your story," Bart said, "aren't they the rocks up at Cougar Point?"

Red Deer looked directly at Bart. "Some say they are. Some say there are scratches on the rocks from the Cougar's claws. I have seen the marks. They are big. I hope I never come across the Cougar that made them." He paused and said, "Now, let us hear your story."

"OK, OK," he bobbed his head as he began. "Now don't any of you expect it to be as good as Red Deer's tales are, but here's some stuff I've learned about the stagecoach robber Black Bart who happens to be my great granddad.

"His real name was Charles E. Boles, and he hailed from Jefferson County, New York. Moved to the Midwest and served with the Illinois Volunteer Infantry during the Civil War a captain. When asked about his education, he answered 'Liberal.' He came out West to make his fortune, in doing so he left his wife, Mary, in Hannibal, Missouri. Some say he tried prospecting, some say he tried retailing, and some say he had a job with Wells Fargo and got fired by an arrogant boss. One thing for sure is he found his calling at robbing stagecoaches, specifically those with Wells Fargo lettered on their sides.

"His robbing days began up north of San Francisco at a spot in the stagecoach line between Point Arenas and Duncan's Mill. That'd be on the Russian River. It was in 1875. Funny thing about Black Bart is he wore mostly white. He always dressed in a long, white coat and put a flour sack over his head, but on top he wore a black derby hat. On that day he stepped out in front of the stagecoach and pointed a double-barrel shotgun at the driver. Then he shouted the words he would use over and over for the next eight years, 'Throw down the box.'

"The driver hesitated for a second, and then Black Bart hollered to the bushes around the stage, 'If he dares shoot, give him a volley.' The coachman looked around and saw what appeared to be several gun barrels aimed at him from the brush. He heaved the strongbox out onto the ground. Black Bart told him to move on.

"A while later, the coachman decided to return to the scene. When he got there, he saw the smashed box on the ground, but he also thought the robbers were still lying in wait for him in the brush because he could still see their gun barrels. But no shots came from them, and he went closer to find only straight sticks pointing at him.

"Black Bart had some tricks up his sleeve. The driver found the strongbox empty. The mysterious band had escaped with $300 in coins and a check for $305.52, drawn on the Granger's Bank of San Francisco. But Black Bart left something behind: a poem penned on the back of a waybill, each line written in a slightly different manner. It read:

"I've labored long and hard for bread --
For honor and for riches --

But on my corns too long you've tred,
You fine-haired sons of bitches.

"It was signed, 'Black Bart, the Po8.'

"Legend has it people were greatly amused by Bart's clean getaway and his Po-8-try. Wells Fargo, however, didn't think it was funny. They put their employees on the lookout for this robber-poet, but their description of him could have fit almost anybody. The Granger's Bank check was never cashed. Bart waited almost a full year before he struck again.

"His next robbery was in the Feather River Valley near Quincy. Again, he told the driver to, 'Throw down the box.' In it was $379 in currency, a diamond ring allegedly worth $200, and a $25 watch.

"The posse that was organized found the box. In it was another poem:

"Here I lay me down to sleep
To wait the coming morrow,
Perhaps success, perhaps defeat,
and everlasting sorrow.

Let come what will I'll try it on,
My condition can't be worse;
And if there's money in that box,
Tis money in my purse!

"Again folks got a laugh, but the Governor of California posted a $300 reward for Bart's capture. Wells Fargo added $300, and the post office added $200. The bounty on his head didn't slow him down, however. Black Bart held up three more stages over the next week, all of them Wells Fargo.

"He stuck to tried-and-true methods. He'd stop the coaches at the crest of steep grades, where horses would be winded and slower than normal. He always used a shotgun, but it was never loaded. He always cut the mail sacks with a "T," and smashed the boxes open.

"Many of his victims described him as a gentleman. A scared woman once tossed Bart her purse, and he returned it to her, saying, 'All's I want is the Wells Fargo strongbox and the mail sack. And he never rode a horse on a robbery! He'd walk! He was quite a mountain man, learned a lot about staying alive while he was a scout in the Army.

"Maybe Bart had a feeling his days were numbered because he quit leaving poems. Too much evidence maybe. He'd probably heard that Wells Fargo was pretty mad at him, had hired a detective named James Hume to track him down and put him in prison. Hume's big break came on what proved to be Black Bart's last holdup.

"In 1883, Black Bart held up a stage headed to Milton. He knew there was gold on board from the Patterson Mine carrying hundreds of dollars in gold. Also on board was a 19-year-old passenger named Jimmy Rolleri. On one steep grade leading around a hill where the horses had to go slow, Rolleri jumped out and decided to do some rabbit hunting.

"At the top of the hill, Black Bart stopped the stage. Bart gave the order to, 'Throw down the box,' but the driver, named McConnell, said there wasn't one on board. Bart knew better, so he ordered McConnell down and told him to unhitch the horses and lead them over the hill. Bart began to search the stage for the box, which he found bolted to the floor.

"McConnell spotted Rolleri coming around the hill with his rifle. He got it and crept back up the road to find Bart backing out of the stagecoach. McConnell shot Black Bart who took off into the brush still holding onto his loot, but he dropped a pack of papers. When McConnell got to the stage, he saw there was fresh blood on the papers.

"Oh, and Black Bart had dropped his derby and failed to pick up some belongings that he'd hidden nearby. There was some food, a pair of field glasses, three dirty linen cuffs, a razor, and a handkerchief full of buckshot. Without too much trouble, the local sheriff found the lady who had sold Bart his provisions. But the clue that broke the Black Bart case wide open was a laundry mark on that abandoned handkerchief: F.X.O.7.

"A short time later, Harry Morse, a special agent on the case, had questioned all of San Francisco's 91 laundries. He found an owner to match that mark: Charles Boles, a 50-year-old resident of the Webb House, at 37 Second Street, Room 40. And talk about your luck coming to an end. While Morse was talking to the laundry owner, guess who walks in. Sure enough, one Charles Boles, who was arrested on the spot.

"Polite and gentlemanly as ever, Boles went along peacefully. At first he denied his wealth was gotten through robbery. He told them he was the owner of a gold mine up in the hills, but people started to identify him, so he took it that one confession to one stage robbery, although he had robbed 27, might get him out of a heap of trouble.

"The judge proved him right, because my great granddaddy got sentenced to six years in San Quenton for robberies that should have gotten him life. As it turned out, he only served four, got off early for good behavior.

"Actually, when he got out, he was quite the dandy. Reporters waited for him as the prison boat brought him ashore. They wanted to know if he were going to rob anymore stagecoaches. 'No gentlemen,' he replied, 'I'm all through with crime.' Another reporter asked if he would write more poetry. He laughed and said, 'Now didn't you hear me say that I am through with crime?' "

Bart grew quiet and dropped his head slightly. "Soon after that, he disappeared forever. At last report, Black Bart was heading south, got as far as Visalia, and then was never seen again." He looked into the campfire and said no more.

"But that ain't the end, now is it, Bart?" spoke up a ranch hand. "What about the $20,000 they've never found?"

Bart chuckled. "It wasn't that much, was it?"

"Seems like that's what I've heard."

He looked at Red Deer and smiled broadly before saying, "Well, the way my granddaddy told it to my daddy, that money was all returned."

The ranch hand laughed heartily. "Yeah, yeah, well that's good. 'Cause nobody likes Wells Fargo anyways. If'n your great-granddaddy got to keep all that money, good for him. And I say good for you, too."

"Thanks," Bart said.

"And we all know how you got even with Wells Fargo, now don't we?" Wally said.

"Yep," Bart answered, "Me and my daddy did pretty well, now didn't we?"

"Modern, highway robbery, is more like it," Whitey yelled. "Whoopee, what I wouldn't do to have the track record you do on Wall Street."

"My dad's idea. I wasn't much to do with it. It was his plan to buy Wells Fargo when it went public."

"But the money, where'd that come from?"

Bart looked at the ranch hand who'd asked the question. "You ask me that all the time, so you know my answer."

"And you're sticking to it, is my guess."

"You got that right."

"Payback is hell. You own the company yet?

"Not hardly."

"Well, let's just hope the stock keeps splitting," Wally let out, "I'm looking for a partner you know." He laughed heartily.

"I'll keep it in mind," Bart replied, "but for now, that's my story. That good for you, Red Deer?"

Red Deer nodded.

"Then it's time for s'mores!" shouted Bitty as she and Rainbow appeared with trays of Graham Crackers, marshmallows, and Hersheys.

Rainbow added, "And after that, I know y'all can use some calories and caffeine to perk you up."

CHAPTER THIRTEEN

The rain rattling on the roof of the cabin played a wicked lullaby for the weary couple. Right after the s'mores had been made and consumed at the bonfire, a rumbling in the distance had rolled over the gathering. Lightning strikes raced across the sky, going sideways, zigzagging wildly, creating fingers of white energy that warned of the approaching storm. Wally and Bitty had quickly packed their guests in the hay wagon and transported them back to the ranch house. By the time they had arrived, a steady shower fell. Beth and Mike's clothes were wet when they'd jumped out of the wagon in front of the Wildcat Cabin.

Now they lay in each other's arms, curled after another session of lovemaking that carried them into a land of bliss. But that state could have been denied easily by Beth, because she held an inward set of emotions that she'd chosen not to address, not to acknowledge, not to let ruin her evening or vacation for that matter. Beth had held her emotions in check, emotions that were flamed when she'd overheard Rainbow's advance to Mike as they'd sat around the bonfire. When she first heard Rainbow come onto Mike, she almost had lost it, lost control and lashed out at the vixen who wanted her man. But instead of making a scene, Beth had let the action play out, and she was happy she had. Mike had rejected Rainbow's come-on, put her down short and sweet. And although Beth had wanted to add her two cents' worth, she was glad she had not. Instead, she'd absorbed the circumstance, mired as it was, and let her man handle it. Much of her happiness was that he had, especially so firmly.

That Rainbow had made the play was also a compliment, as Beth saw it. Beth had known that Mike was desirable, had obviously known it since they had become a couple that seven years ago. And Beth still desired him, obviously, but it was nice to have someone else desire him. It was kind of an affirmation that Mike was still a catch, and that Beth had made a good choice.

So last night when her blood was about to boil out of her veins, Beth had let it go, had simply trusted that Mike would do right. That he had was even more reason for Beth to be happy with her decision. Knowing she could trust him was such a wonderful feeling.

When they'd stripped out of their wet clothes, the welt on his thigh was immediately apparent, and although Beth could have ignored bringing it up, she'd said, "Wow, that mosquito really bit you!"

"Yes," Mike had replied, "and I'm very glad to have squished it." He stood nude in front of her and ran his finger over the swelling.

"Me, too." She put her hand on it, her warm palm flush on his cool skin. Another swelling close to the spot immediately caught her attention. "What have we here?" she'd cooed as she ran her hand further up his thigh.

"Oh, that's my little stinger."

"I'd never call it little, Sexy Man," were her words as nature took it course, one that led them to bed.

Now much later, awake and listening to the tympany pound on the roof, Beth was very happy at her decision.

In deep sleep, Mike was also happy. The whole affair had taken him aback. He'd known of Rainbow's reputation, but her blatant approach was hard to believe. Though it was flattering to have a woman as stunning as she was to make such a suggestion, he was really put off by it. First off, her nerve approached conceit; and secondly, he was totally committed to another woman, pure and simple. Rainbow was way out of line with her action, and if they'd been somewhere less public, somewhere where he could have raised his voice, he would have taken an even more direct approach to put her in her place.

And then when he and Beth were back in the cabin, removing their wet clothes, when she had pointed out the red mark left by Rainbow's pinch, he had almost told her what had happened. In one respect, it would have cleared his conscience and offered him a chance to talk about it, but in another way, it would have complicated things greatly. After all, they were having such a wonderful vacation, both mentally and physically, and he didn't want to spoil it. So when Beth had put her hand on him, when it caused such an immediate arousal in him which prompted her to take matters into her hands, he decided to let Rainbow's words and actions go, and every inch of him, high and wide, inside and out, conscious and asleep, was happy he had.

Beth listened to Mike's breathing, ran her hand over his salt and pepper hair, took a whiff of Kouros that lingered on his skin, and said a silent prayer of thanks for having him in her life. This trip and some time away from Milford had been exactly what she'd needed. She closed her eyes and welcomed sleep to take her. It did, pulling her down, pulling her into a calm, pulling her into a state of comfort only someone who was in love could know.

The pounding on the door snatched both of them back to reality.

"Mike! Mike and Beth!" a familiar voice called out. The rain was still banging on the roof. "A flash of lightning lit the room, and the subsequent thunder drowned out the summons from Bart at the door.

"Mike!" Bart yelled. With a gloved fist, he banged on the door again. "Hey, get up! I need your help. Mike! Beth!"

"It's Bart," Beth said to Mike.

"Hold on!" Mike shouted as he threw off the sheet and swung his legs over the side of the bed. "I'm coming."

The pounding continued.

"Coming!" Mike repeated, grabbing his pants and pulling them on. He walked to the door and flipped on the porch light. "Bart, what's the matter?"

"We got a situation brewing," the foreman answered. "There's a flood coming."

The rain had been steady, but it was never torrential, as Mike saw it. "A flood? This has hardly even been a thunderstorm!" he said, although as soon as he had gotten the words out a streak of lightning and clap of thunder came down simultaneously just a short distance away.

"We ain't got much rain here," Bart explained, "but up in the mountains, where the stream comes from, they got a downpour. There's cattle we got to move, and we'd like your help."

"Mine?" Mike asked.

"You ride real well. Another hand would make a big difference, really."

"How about Beth?"

"She can come along if she wants. But she don't have to." Bart let the words lie, then said, "And you don't have to either, if you don't want. It might be dangerous. But you'd be a real help. A big help."

In a robe, Beth came to the door and said, "Hi, Bart. Got a problem, huh?"

"Yes, Beth. We've got some work to do. I'm asking Mike if he wants to help."

"I heard."

"You, too, if you want."

"Rainbow going to be there?" Beth asked.

"Definitely."

She replied, "We'll be there as soon as we can get dressed."

"We'll have your horses ready. Plan on getting wet."

Beth and Mike were not the only creatures abruptly roused from their quarters on this menacing morning. Eyes accustomed to peering through darkness looked out into the night to see the torrential rain falling in silvery sheets. This was a new dwelling in an old territory. The former den, not far away, was tucked under a huge, downed tree, but had fallen prey to termites. After surveying the area for a place to relocate, this spot had seemed ideal. First off, it was big enough to house his six feet of tightly muscled body. Next, because it was high above the stream, only a sure-footed animal could reach it. The ledge that jutted over it assured no attack could come from above. The interior promised to be cool in summer, and with some adept preparation would be warm in winter. The entrance was tilted such that any intruder could be seen easily if it tried to enter.

This was to be home, but now as water increasing flowed across the floor from the back of the lair, it was obvious another new, drier space would have to be located and quickly, because if there was anything he did not like, it was getting wet for no reason. He peered out into the bleak darkness and let out a low growl that made the rock under his paws vibrate. He was not a happy cat.

CHAPTER FOURTEEN

Wet was not exactly the correct term, as it turned out. Drenched was what they were. Riding slowly on their horses along the muddy trail leading to the pastures, everyone, no matter what they were wearing, was soaked to the bone. "At least it's a warm rain," Wally offered for comfort.

Beth felt none, however, with water dripping off her hat and running down her back. Neither did the others as they moved out in the pre-dawn hours to do a task that was never much fun, coaxing cattle that they should be somewhere they weren't. At the end of the fence row, the group broke into two, with Wally leading one and Bart the other.

Wally's outfit was comprised of Whitey and several ranch hands. They were going to go upstream where there was a small bridge which they would cross. The herd of cattle they were checking on would be driven to higher ground where a fenced pasture would keep them away from the flooding Wally expected on the lowlands along the waterway.

Bart's gang was made up of Mike, Beth, and Rainbow. Their task was more select. They were to go to the mountains and make sure none of the cattle had ventured from the upper pasture.

At first, Wally had thought Bart would ride the lower plain, but Bart had insisted on going the mountain route. "We can ride fast and get there and be done with it quickly," he'd reasoned. "When we finish, we'll come down and help you."

Wally finally agreed. At least Bart was only taking a

small crew, two of which were new to the range. With Rainbow along, the job would be manageable. If only they didn't start arguing and fighting. With that in mind, Wally figured that maybe he really didn't want the two of them along with him anyway. "Get done and get back as soon as you can," he told them. "We don't want to lose any cattle!"

At the end of the fence, the groups split, and as fast as their horses could carry them in the mud and precipitation, they rode. Beth and Mike had been over the same ground before, but with rain coming down nearly sideways, the view was nothing at all like it was when they were meandering along on their way to a picnic. Bart led the charge, almost at a full gallop, only held back by the chance of unsure footing and inexperienced riders. He had them follow him on the trail, shouting orders at the top of his lungs to caution them of hazards along the way. Ultimately, he trusted the mounts they rode, because the horses would follow their instincts, which Bart knew were better than his.

Lightning flashed across the dark sky, lighting it up and making the ground look like it was electrified. The horses were not phased. Thunder clapped so close it shook the earth. The horses kept their pace. The wind threw pellets of rain as big as dimes into their faces. The horses galloped on.

Even though the gang was hampered by climatic elements that would have sent most people looking for cover, they still forged onward and made good time. What had taken several hours on their previous journey took less than an hour today.

None of them acknowledged aloud that they were passing Cougar Point, but each in the quartet recognized the configuration of rocks and was surprised at how fast it had appeared. They continued riding. They entered the forest and hurried up the trail, all the while traveling single file. In a matter of moments, Bart twisted around on his saddle and shouted, "We've got to slow down. It could get a little slick through here."

Beth, remembering her slip the last time they had come to the cabin, breathed a sigh of relief. Several times during the rapid ride over, she had battled to keep her balance and could only be grateful to the fates that she hadn't fallen off. She silently welcomed the slowdown.

Likewise, Mike was thankful to have slowed down, especially on this narrow, slippery trail. Although the rain's onslaught was slightly broken by the overhead canopy of trees, the deluge, nevertheless, came down, with some drops even bigger as they were formed through their capture by tree boughs, only to be released after they had teamed with others.

Fortunately for the four humans, the horses kept their composure, moving ahead with confidence and poise. Fortunately for the horses, the four people were doing likewise.

They came to a little clearing, and Bart slowed and pointed, then yelled, "Indian Lookout."

The site was barely familiar, and certainly nowhere near what it looked like the other day. Visibility was nil. Against the rain, a silvery mist fought its way up the mountainside. The view was of clouds, roiling, rolling, billowing, ballooning, dirty-white, unrelenting, angry vapors whipped about by a biting wind.

Beth remembered that she could see for miles the other day, as far as the ranch house, but today, even as the sky was lightening in hue, signaling the sun had risen, there was nothing pretty about it as she looked out beyond the cliff and hoped what Wally and the others far below were safe.

They decreased their speed once again as they wound their way up into the trees where the trail narrowed again. They went a bit further and turned to the left. The sound was deafening. Following the stream now, Mike recalled that it had been some 30 yards below them the other day. Today it looked like it had more than tripled its size and nearly filled the entire hollow. The whole area looked like a pot of boiling, muddy water.

Trying to remain on the graveled path, now itself ushering a stream of water some three inches deep, became the main focus in all their lives. Up until that moment, when he looked down and saw the rushing water, what they were doing had been a little bit fun to Mike, a little bit exciting. But now, as he looked in front of Thunder's head and saw Beth atop Freckles, he knew that what they were doing was very dangerous and extremely serious.

It made him wonder if he was ready. It made him question his strength. It cut to his gut and made him ask, *What would I do if I lost her? What if I never could see her smile, touch her face, her skin?* His heart began to race as thoughts of never inhaling Euphoria on her skin, seeing her blue/green eyes sparkle, running his hands through her auburn hair filled his mind. He called out to her, "Beth!" but at that exact moment a flash of lightning accompanied by thunder filled the air. Across the stream bank they could see a tree trunk explode like a firecracker.

The sight and sound caused them all to stop for a second. Behind Mike, where Rainbow rode, he could hear Beauty whinny. He turned around and saw the jet black animal rear up, its hooves no more than five feet from Thunder's rear end.

"Whoa, whoa, girl!" Rainbow shouted.

What happened next might have been considered humorous if it were a scene from a slap-stick comedy, but in real life, it was anything but funny. When Beauty's hooves came down, one of them nicked Thunder's hind quarter, which startled him and sent him bounding forward. Instantly, he bumped into Freckles, and she was goosed into motion. Freckles' advance spooked Bullet, who jumped forward in a panic. Luckily, Mike, Beth, and Bart were able to hold on as their horses raced up the slope.

Rainbow was not as fortunate. When Beauty's front feet hit the ground, she immediately reared up again, Rainbow, an excellent equestrian, went with the motion, and under normal circumstances would have easily managed to regain control. But with the rain coming down, the wet saddle, the narrow path, the incline, the physical intensity of the action, Rainbow was thrown off. She landed on the trail. Once there, she rolled ever so slightly to her left, a move that saved her from being trampled by Beauty's feet. But it was also a move that caused her to slide off the edge and tumble down the side of the mountain. If the other riders were within earshot, they would have heard her screaming for help.

A bit further up, the trail curved to the right, where it met the once flat stream bed, once a mere ten feet across, once only a few inches deep, once the headwater for a picturesque waterfall, once a clear flow of cool water beckoning horses to take a drink and riders to wipe their brows. Now it was a rampaging rapid more than double its normal size. A three-foot rush of water now raged over the edge, creating a massive waterfall that roared over the rocky ledges and crashed into a bubbling basin below.

The three horses and riders stopped just short of the torrent. They were all agitated, all shook up, all straining for control and somehow finding it.

Mike dared to look down. The brownish green water looked like a huge sea monster writhing in front of them. The sound was everywhere. He looked up at Bart and could see he was saying something but could not hear it. "What?" Mike yelled.

Bart forced Bullet to back up and yelled again, "Where's Rainbow?"

Just able to hear, Mike shouted back, "Don't know!" and hunched his shoulders. At that very moment, Beauty dashed by them, sans Rainbow, and lunged into the rampant water.

Mike and Beth saw it happen and gasped.

Bart saw it happen and sent himself into the fury. He went after Beauty. He dug his heels into Bullet's flanks and shot forward, meeting the force of the water just as Beauty's momentum had carried her through to the other side. With every ounce of his strength, with his calves and his thighs, with his arms, his hands, from his fingers to his toes, Bart coordinated every muscle in his body and tried to stay on Bullet.

Man and horse hit the current almost at full speed. Bullet's forelegs splashed in, touched bottom, and as soon as his rear legs found support, the front legs rose from the water.

Bullet was a strong animal; so was Bart, for that matter, and together they made a powerful team, but they were no match for the force of nature they were pitted against. Whereas Beauty was running at full speed with no weight on her back, Bullet was close but not fully there. Adding the weight of the man he carried, the water was too much. Bullet's body twisted, his back legs slipped to the left, he toppled into the raging stream, and before either Mike or Beth could move a muscle, both Bart and Bullet were swept over the edge. The last thing they saw was Bart's hat as it spun briefly in the mist made by the falls before following its owner.

Mike looked at Beth. She looked at him. They both looked at the spot where they'd last seen Bart. They looked down the trail to the spot where they'd last seen Rainbow. They looked at each other.

"What are we going to do?" she cried out to him over the roar of water.

He could not hear her. He dismounted, motioning for her get down off of Freckles. He still held Thunder's reins, actually held them up to show her to do the same.

Immediately she went to him.

He wrapped his arms around her. For the longest moment, they stood there holding each other.

Beth was the first to speak. "I'm so happy it wasn't you."

Recalling the last thought he'd had before the tragedy started, he replied, "I'm happy it wasn't you." He tightened his arms.

Beth let his strength flow over her. "Mike, what are we going to do?" she asked.

His reply was, "Look for them."

"Look for them? Do you see that current?" she said incredulously. "How can we fight that?"

"I don't know, but we've got to try." He backed her away with his hands and looked into her blue/green eyes. "Before it's too late."

"Should one of us go for help?" she suggested.

"First we've got to look for them," he answered.

Water still ran from the back wall of the den. The

cougar sat at its entrance on the middle of a huge slab of stone where his feet would remain dry. His tail wrapped around his body. The sun had risen, but the storm had not lessened. Wind rushed down the hollow, bending tree limbs and bushes, whipping up leaves and twigs. The sudden deluge of mud and rocks that swept in front of him was greatly unexpected, especially when it was followed by a whinnying equine beast thrashing its legs in an attempt to stop its fall.

Immediately the cougar crouched, partly in defense but mostly to prepare for action. He craned his neck forward to survey the land beneath. The horse had plunked into the water some 10 yards below. A quick look downstream revealed another creature, a human half submerged in the raging water, clinging to a fallen tree. The cougar's sensitive auditory receptive system zeroed in on the high-pitched screams for help. This was highly unusual. This might call for getting a little wet.

Bart's tumble over the ledge could easily have killed him. In fact, at any other time when the water was moving at a normal rate, it probably would have. However, the volume of liquid rushing over the edge threw him out further than normal. His path carried him beyond the sharp rocks protruding along the rock face. His body was like a huge cork as he fell down to the massive basin of swirling water. Making a splash that was hardly worth noting, he landed feet first, and went right to the bottom, where his strength and stamina paid off. He was able to gulp a lungful of air before he hit, and while he was tumbled and thrown about underwater, while he was bashed into submerged roots and sucked down when he tried to swim up, while he kicked with all his might and clawed at the water with his massive hands, through all of this, he never ran out of air. Nevertheless, when his head did pop up, he wasted no time drawing in what he knew was the most precious breath he'd taken since possibly his birth.

He faced the falls, and when he looked up into the pounding rain, he could only guess how lucky he was to have survived. Hurriedly he checked his limbs. Everything seemed OK. He was being drawn downstream by the current. To see where he was going, maybe even catch a glimpse of where Rainbow might be, he turned around, and right then he came face to face with the side of a branch-like root sticking out from the bank. He threw his hands up to protect himself. In the process, his right elbow became wedged in a fork in the root. His forehead smashed with a resounding thud against the slick surface of the root, and his body was washed underneath it. Fortunately, the trapped elbow kept his mouth above water, saving him from drowning.

Rainbow clung to the log with all her might. The fall down the mountainside had torn her skin, ripped her clothing, and bruised her body. She too suffered no broken bones, but her muscles were battered and a deep gash along her side caused pain like she had never known before. Her right cheek was swelling badly after she'd bounced face first off a rock. The pain was moving over her like a fingers of frost growing on a window pane. She hurt so bad that she stopped screaming. Her head was throbbing, mostly from landing on her neck in a net of wild grapes which caught her just before she would have struck the tree trunk she now held onto. For a few seconds, the vines had supported her, then they slowly began to snap and separate. Fighting through her pain, she'd twisted her torso and flexed her knees and legs so she was able to rest on her back.

Then all of a sudden, her butt slipped through and she'd found herself in the cold water. Instantly she'd reached up, in much the same reaction that Bart would use, and clutched at the log. She'd had the strength to scream then. She'd screamed for help with every ounce of energy she had. Her fingers had found a broken branch to grab; they'd found a bit of wisteria vine to seize. The current had pulled her body downstream. She'd held on. She'd opened her mouth to yell again, but the liquid swept in and quelled her cries and her spirit. The water was cold. It numbed her body, but the result was welcome, because it took away her pain. She closed her eyes from which warm tears mixed with the flood washing around her.

This was not at all like the day he'd expected. When it had begun raining, he'd been satisfied his choice of a new home was a good one. He'd slept instead of hunting last night, cozy in the back of his lair. Then being rudely awakened by water seeping into his nest had really turned his mood. His life was reactionary, but the thought of having to find another place to stay was unsettling. Then came the cloudburst that filled the hollow. He sensed that prey would be hard to find for quite some time. Then the equine animal fell past his door. Unfortunately, once it hit the water, it swam to the other bank and high-tailed it away down the valley. Then the appearance of the screaming human, which for some time now had appeared lifeless. This looked to be the time to get wet.

"Please, Mike, be careful," Beth pleaded as he inched his way down the bank. With one hand, he held onto the rope that they'd fastened to a tree along the side of the trail. With the other, he felt his way down the embankment. Beth was but a few feet above him, carefully moving toward the stream that held both Rainbow and Bart in its clutches.

From their position, they could see both bodies in the water. They chose going to Rainbow first for one simple reason: it looked plausible. Bart's plight, on the other hand, was a different matter. Reaching him looked nearly impossible from the trail. Mike and Beth could only hope that an avenue for his rescue materialized once they had reached the bottom of the hollow.

Although the rain still came down, it was definitely slowing. That would not affect the stream, they realized, but would probably help with visibility. And it was surprising to find that even with the amount of rain that had fallen, the ground was not saturated. Instead, when Mike dug his fingers into the earth, trying to stabilize his decent, he'd found the ground dry a few inches deep.

Slowly, deliberately, they proceeded closer toward Rainbow. Her arms hung over the log. Her face was turned from them, pressed to the grey-brown wood. Her matted, auburn hair, littered with twigs and bits of leaves, flowed behind her in the muddy water. Her form was lifeless, and they could only hope they were not too late.

Upstream was Bart, in nearly the same position, only he was on his back, floating atop the current, his arm stretched behind. It was plain that he was trapped. He appeared to be unconscious. They knew they had to hurry.

But both Mike and Beth knew they had to proceed with caution. Although they wanted to move faster, there was no reason to rush and risk having an accident themselves. They knew two others' lives were depending on them. With intentional, calculating steps, they continued.

In creeping, crawling steps, the cougar moved slowly also. He'd slipped beneath his den and stole along the stream bank, just above the water level. From rock to rock he approached. His skill was to be silent, invisible, undetected until the last possible moment. Then the utmost advantage, surprise, was his.

Without so much as snapping a twig, he went forward paw by paw. With every step his prey became bigger and bigger, and in his mind, so did he.

"Do you think she's alive?" Beth finally worked up the courage to ask Mike. They were within ten yards of Rainbow and had stopped to look over the area.

"I can't tell," replied Mike. He leaned his head forward to try to get a better look. "She might be."

"Oh, I'm scared," Beth admitted. "What if she'd

dead?" She put her hand on Mike's arm and squeezed it.

He looked into her blue/green eyes but did not speak.

"That could have been you!" Her voice was strained.

"I know," he responded. "Or you, and I swear, I don't know how I'd be acting right now if it were."

"I could have lost you like that." She said in a whisper. "It happened so fast. I still can't believe it."

He drew her near, held her in his arms and said into her auburn hair. "That's how life is, isn't it? Here today and gone tomorrow."

"One second is more like it." She drew back to see his blue eyes. "I hope I haven't given you the impression I take you for granted. I know sometimes I get a little preoccupied, and I don't think of you as much as I should. But I do cherish being with you."

"I know, and you are everything to me. And I know I'm just as guilty as you." He glanced down at Rainbow then back at Beth. "To think, it happened just like that." He snapped his fingers.

Even though the roar of the water filled the hollow with a deafening sound, the Cougar's ears were much more than human. The snap made by Mike's fingers shot a ripple through the animal's body which caused an instant response. He bound from his spot under the rock and lunged onto the fallen log sticking out over the stream. The human's body was but a few feet away, and soon it would be his. He would tolerate no other taking claim to his feast.

The flash of cashmere feline in front of them caused both Beth and Mike to fall backward against the bank. Clinging to each other, they watched as the huge cat pounced on the log and swished its tail back and forth as it watched Rainbow's body move in the water. They held their breath as the cat placed one massive paw in front of the other, delicately stalking its way forward.

While they watched in silence, the cougar soon stood right over Rainbow's head. It bent down and sniffed the human's scent.

Beth found the strength to whisper, "What now?"

"You go help Rainbow," Mike said with authority.

Beth looked at him, eyebrows raised, her blue/green eyes open wide, and said, "What?"

"You go help her, get her out of the water," Mike ordered her.

"And what about that cougar?"

"Leave the cougar to me," he said, then turned to her and pulled her to him. He kissed her and uttered, "Just know that I love you." With that, he pushed himself up and yelled at the top of his lungs, "Rainbow! Rainbow, look here! Hey, wake up and look here." He jumped up and down and waved his hands back and forth above his head. Then he dug his feet into the ground and began to run, shouting as he did, "Hey, yeaooouuuuu!" and then again, "Yeaooouuuuu!" as he raced along the stream bank upstream, struggling to keep his balance and consciously shouting at the top of his lungs to attract the cougar's attention.

His plan worked.

The cat's head snapped up, and his eyes immediately zeroed in on the form moving through the under-brush. With incredible quickness, he spun around on the log, hooked his claws into the soft wood, and sprang from the log in one leap and set out to overtake Mike.

Beth watched it all happen as if in slow motion. Her first reaction was to chase after Mike, but she remembered his words, "Help Rainbow." Lest his intent be lost, as fast as her feet could carry her, Beth scurried down the bank and made her way out on the log. Once there, she grabbed at the material on Rainbow's back and pulled her out of the water. The sight of Rainbow's face, scraped, puffy, bruised and raw, nearly made Beth throw up. The sheer sound of pain Rainbow let out provoked a similar feeling.

Through slits of eyelids, Rainbow mumbled, "Mike?"

For a split second, Beth had the notion to let Rainbow go, let her fall into the water and never have to confront or explain again her questionable morals, but the feeling passed. In so many ways, Rainbow was pathetic. Beth heaved and struggled, finally managing to get Rainbow fully from the water, off the log, and onto dry land where the battered woman collapsed and passed out. Beth's attention promptly shifted upstream where she peered for any signs of her man.

Mike had launched his plan knowing fully that it was improbable that it would work to his advantage. Nevertheless, he had always prided himself as a man of action, and could not stand by and watch Rainbow be devoured by a wild animal. He had surprise on his side, he figured, and any advantage was better than none.

Mike had moved quickly through the bush, but, of course, the cougar was quicker. The cat also could maneuver its six-foot frame like a four-legged, two-hundred pound snake through terrain that was its home. In most respects, Mike had no chance, except chance itself.

Thrashing through the limbs and branches, Mike dared not look back. *Where should I go? What should I do?* and similar questions shot through his mind. The water was to his left, the rock face to his right. Ahead? Life. Behind: death. He rushed forward. All he could hear was the roar of the falls and the beating of his heart. If I'm ever going to have a heart attack, it's going to be now, he thought, then felt the world fall out from under him.

At that exact moment, the cat gathered all its strength and sprang at Mike's shoulders, only to its surprise found itself staring into the splintered end of a tree branch. The human was no where to be seen, and the cat reached out with its paw just in time to save it from plunging neckfirst into the sharp barbs.

As it turned out, a sharp splinter caught the skin of the cat's shoulder, ripping it open. "Whreeowww," it cried as its skin split. His system was now supercharged with anger.

Mike's feet fell into water, which saved his head from the cat's claws. A gully full of runoff caught him and sent him toward the overflowing stream. His entrance came with a splash at a point just upstream from where Bart was snagged. In a matter of seconds, Mike was there, and he reached up and grabbed onto the branch-like root.

Bart was still unconscious, his body a limp rag fish-tailing in the water. Mike rested next to him and breathed a sigh of relief. He pulled his body up slightly out of the current and looked downstream to see that Beth and Rainbow were not on the log. He looked around, and although he wasn't sure what had happened to the cougar, he felt his confidence rise. That was a mistake. Mike turned his attention to Bart, trying to figure out how to get him loose.

In positioning his body to free Bart, he did not notice the root dip and shake. He did notice the blood-curdling scream. Mike jerked his head up and saw the fangs, tongue and mouth of the cougar, all the way back to the pink and black skin of its throat. Mike nearly fainted.

The cougar let loose another roar, this one fully meaning, "I'm the boss around here!"

In an instant, Mike saw the cat lift its right paw. It was the size of a catcher's mitt. The feline drew it back, curling his arm upward where it held the position for what seemed like eternity. The claws were fully extended. As if the world was in freeze frame, Mike saw the muscles in the cat's limb tense and watched as the paw began to come forward.

Then, fully wishing that time would stand still, Mike saw the cat's body jerk and then rocket violently from the branch and land limp in the water not a yard from where he and Bart shared the exposed root. The water swiftly devoured the creature.

Mike looked around. Up on the trail he saw Wally standing with a rifle.

After the four of them had been brought up the hillside, Wally took them to the cabin where they could be attended to. Bullet, it seems, had run back down the trail where he was seen by Wally and his crew who figured something was wrong and came to check it out.

It turned out that Bart had a dislocated shoulder, but in true cowboy fashion, pushed aside any offers of assistance, directing all help to Rainbow instead. The gratitude, and yes, the love for Bart, showed in her eyes.

Wally dabbed a swab on Rainbow's cheek and said to Beth and Mike, "I can never repay you. You saved my little girl, and I'll never forget it."

Mike looked at Wally, then at Beth, and the happy couple looked back at Wally and said as one, "Neither will we."

SHARE THE ROMANCE

Each of our personalized romance novels offers a different setting, story line and unique romantic adventure. We welcome you to order our other books and pass this information along to friends who would love to star in a book!

Our novels make one-of-a-kind gifts for Valentine's, birthdays, weddings, anniversaries, Mother's Day or anytime to say "I love you."

• *Another Day in Paradise* takes place at a lavish, new Caribbean resort where our couple are pampered as the honored guests. While exploring their paradise, they stumble onto a danger that threatens to keep them apart. Ultimately, they find it's not money or fame, but love that matters.

• *Love's Bounty: An Outer Banks Romance* is set on the barrier islands of North Carolina's Outer Banks. Our couple explore attractions like Cape Hatteras Lighthouse, the Wright Brothers' Memorial, and *The Lost Colony* outdoor drama. Through an adventure true to Outer Banks' tradition, they rediscover that love conquers all.

• *Cold Feet, Warm Heart* has a cold-weather setting with plenty of warm-blooded action. Our couple visit a ski resort where they're the last to arrive before a blizzard closes the area. Under the instruction of a former, Austrian ski-team member, they can do no wrong until an earth-shattering ordeal provides the true lesson of love.

• *Awake, My Love* occurs in your own town and is a romp back in time. Due to a car accident, our couple get an answer to the question, "What would happen if you lost everything?" Through dream sequences, he becomes a cowboy, she a Miss Kitty in the Old West; she a medieval princess, he her defender; plus much, much more.

• *Sea Double: A Cruise Romance* is set aboard a cruise ship. Our heroine is called upon to switch places with a music-industry mega-star; our hero becomes her bodyguard. Both play at Caribbean ports-of-call like St. Lucia, Curaçao and St. Martin, and bask in first-class comfort, only to find that along with celebrity comes a price.

• *Another Night in Paradise* is set on a mythical Caribbean island. Our couple find a meteorite worth beaucoups bucks and a yacht full of bad guys willing to kill for it. All this after a stellar night of lovemaking under a sky filled with shooting stars amid a tropical world of romance and discovery.

• *Island of Love* takes place in Tahiti, the Island of Love, where the action and romance are of volcanic proportion. Black pearls, black-sand beaches, and the black hearts of villains all play a role. From a cruise ship, our duo ultimately find their destiny rests in myth as deep as the blue Polynesian waters.

• *Away on the Range* is set at a dude ranch on the wide-open plains. The action centers around horses, tall-tales, and pleasures of the wild, with romance coming in the most unexpected places. From outward beauty to inward understanding, the lesson learned is as old as the Wild West.

• *Cruise Alaska* is set in some of the most pristine wilderness left on earth - the Inside Passage with ports like Vancouver, Ketchikan, Juneau and Skagway. Bald eagles, Humpback whales, and the Northern Lights all enter the action before that shining, yellow temptress of the Yukon and her associated evil – gold fever – reveal a deeper meaning.

• *Celebrating Romance* is a collection of 10 romantic, short stories selected as winners in yournovel.com's first Romance Writing Contest held to celebrate our tenth year of business. There's something for everyone with settings that include Paris, a mountain retreat, Acapulco, the Southwest, Barcelona, Maui, Oahu, and even outer space.

• *For the Ages* is set at the Grove Park Inn Resort in Asheville, NC. Our couple visit during autumn's "leaf season," and an insightful guide accompanies them back in time where they meet some of the historic Inn's notable guests such as Thomas Edison, Harry Houdini and F. Scott Fitzgerald. Even the Pink Lady, the resort's resident ghost, plays into what they learn about life and love.

• *Let the Good Times Roll* is set in New Orleans. Our couple find that phrase multiplied during their Mardi Gras visit. They explore the French Quarter, watch parades, catch beads, and ride on a float during the Orpheus Parade. In the prickly heat of the voodoo-laced Big Easy, an itchy situation shows how dear their life together really is.

• *The Treasure Seekers* by Marcy Thomas is set in Fort Lauderdale, where the starring couple go on a treasure hunt. Following clues, they enjoy area attractions and pursue their passion, but coincidence pits them against piracy. Combining their enduring love and a little luck, the couple beat the odds and learn about life's most precious treasure.

• *Shore Thing* features four short stories at four exotic beaches. Little Palm Island in the Florida Keys provides old-fashioned romance and a spooky encounter. Fiji's Beachcomber Island proves the present even better than the "good old days." The cliffside Reefs property Bermuda leads to sudden drama. And Peter Island in the British Virgin Islands offers an unforgettable night under the stars.

• *Heart of the Keys* by Marcy Thomas is set in Key West. The US's "Southernmost City" provides more than the usual excitement for the starring couple in this outrageous romantic romp. A love letter written in 1848 holds a secret to be unraveled in this tale of elusive love and everlasting romance.

• *New Mexico Nights* features desert and mountain grandeur, the light that's inspired countless artists, and more in this tale that's as hot as local chile peppers. Albuquerque's hot-air ballooning, Taos' natural hot springs, and Santa Fe's art galleries all lead to an inspiration of an unusual nature that puts an unexpected price on our couple's escapade.

• *Rome: Diamonds, Danger and Desire* by Marcy Thomas is a sexy European adventure, where the starring male takes on the role of a secret agent. He and his special lady hang out with mysterious types, including a sultan who plans to purchase the world's most perfect diamond. A colorful gang of thieves has other ideas for the gem. Against the backdrop of the Coliseum, the Vatican and all that Rome has to offer comes an intriguing tale of love, adventure and heroics.

• *Jamaica Rendezvous: A Couples Ocho Rios Romance* is set at Jamaica's first all-inclusive resort for couples only. Our couple indulge in all the resort has to offer, which includes horseback riding, snorkeling, and sailing, and are taught a lesson of love, courtesy of an ocean treasure. Hot nights, exotic entertainment, and passionate encounters make theirs a vacation to remember.

• *Season's Greetings, Season's Love* by Marcy Thomas is set in the town of Harmony where the winter holidays are a time of enchantment and celebration. Our starring couple find quaint shops, friendly people, and a snow-covered landscape. But when an unexpected turn of events tests the fabric of this utopian village, will life and love ever be the same?

• The *"I Love You" Coupon Book* and the *"I Love You, Mom" Coupon Book* are also available.

800-444-3356
yournovel.com
3100 Arrowwood Drive
Raleigh, NC 27604

ORDER#: 38159